# JUEGO DE CHICOS

# JUEGO DE CHICOS

## Facundo R. Soto

Translated by
Abel M. Folgar

Jitney Books

Juego de Chicos by Facundo R. Soto
Translated from Spanish by Abel M. Folgar
Copyright © 2018

Published by Jitney Books

Printed in the United States of America

Front cover art by Aquarela Sabol
Interior lay out by J.J. Colagrande
Jitney books logo by Ahol Sniffs Glue
Front cover design by Marlene Lopez
Author photo by Claudia Jares

Jitney Books is a Miami-based micro-publishing company focused on producing
original titles by Miami-based authors writing about Miami in Miami with the
intention of this material being produced into film or plays by Miami-based
filmmakers or playwrights. All cover art will feature Miami-based artists.

Please contact publisher for media, acquisition and collaboration inquiries:

jitneybooks@gmail.com

@jitneybooks

#MADEINDADE

#MIAMIFULLTIME

# JUEGO DE CHICOS

# FOREWORD:

I have been a lifelong lover of football (soccer) and was excited to be a part of the translation effort when Yago S. Cura first told me about it in the spring of 2017. Yago's a poet and librarian with the Los Angeles Public Library and had the opportunity to meet Facundo while attending the *Feria Internacional del Libro de Buenos Aires* in a professional capacity the previous year. This turned to friendship and in turn, into the translated work you now hold. I had no idea what I signed on for but my friendship with Yago dates back to the mid-90's when we were both college students at Florida International University and in the nascent days of our forays into poetics. Our bond has been strong since—built upon poetry and football.

On my first read of the Spanish text I was blown away by the visceral sexual overtones of the narrative—had I gotten myself into queer erotica somehow? I was wrong. After learning of Facundo's background as a psychologist, I saw the book differently. This was a demystification of machismo. This was a book about sports with the requisite "locker room" talk; a hot topic in the current political climate of the United States, but not one I had ever been exposed to. If you sub out the objects of desire, you're in familiar territory.

Beyond the idea of a group of gay men playing in an organized league in Argentina, which I found a fascinating proposition given the South American nation's fervent zealotry over the sport and the intrinsic macho image of the Latin male, I saw Miami in it too. David Beckham's years-long fight to get an MLS franchise in South Florida has finally become a reality. I can only guess that he finally figured out that he had to grease the right hands and line the influential pockets first. Since I've resided here, it has always been a mystery as to why there isn't more footie going on. It must be because of Miami's transient and *cambia chaqueta* attitude towards sports. This town sucks in the dry years. The Miami Dolphins, HEAT and Marlins—championship franchises in their respective leagues, can hardly draw a crowd well into playoff scenarios—what will an MLS team do?

The Miami Fusion couldn't. The Miami FC did less and their league, the NASL, just folded their entire 2018 season. The Toros barely lasted four years in the 70's. There's the argument that South Florida's population is comprised of a large population of Latin American transplants and it's true. Latin Americans who rep their home clubs and national teams. Latin Americans who sadly, couldn't give a shit about a team here. And yet, the parks are full every weekend and most weekday nights. Lord knows that on good weeks, I play at least three times. There's an interest here.

And then there's Miami's niche in the gay world. Miami Beach has long been associated with the LGBTQ scene. How is it so, I've always wondered? Against the backdrop of one of the most macho cities in the US? I don't have answers for this. I find the abraxas-like duality of Miami's acknowledgement/denial interesting. What I would find even more interesting, would be an LGBTQ league of footie aficionados taking off in the Magic City—that would make sense to me. According to the rules of Facundo's team, I'd be able to join, so long as I show effort on the pitch and refrain from cutting my dick off. Fair enough. This is a lesson in diversity and tolerance that I think we can all understand, and relate to.

**Abel M. Folgar,**
**Miami, FL 2018**

## NOTES ON THE TRANSLATION AND TRANSLATORS:

The project was originally conceived to mimic the way the book is written: like a game day roster call-up sheet. Yago assembled a group of US-based writers to translate the chapters. Like all teams cobbled together during the summer transfer months, there were complications. Once we decided to buckle down and get this puppy together, we had a nice co-ed team to work the chapters. Yago translated "Turquesa," "The Game on TV," "Blood in the Eye" and "He's Coming on a Motorcycle." Claudia D. Hernandez translated "Two Lovers" and Taca Albarracín translated "When Molecular Food is Transformed into Hotdogs," "The Doc's Idea," "The Son of the Military Man" and "Plastic Dreams." I translated the rest. Without their hard work and commitment, this translation and editing job would've been impossible. We are all Spanish-speakers, some Argentine even; but knowing that not all Spanish is the same, I decided to keep a "middle of the road" attitude towards the *sense* of certain words rooted in the Latin American version of the language. To me, it's *un perro, la mafafa*. To Facundo *un pancho, un faso*. To you, it's a hotdog, some weed. I also opted to keep the style of his writing, his lines and dialogue breaks as they appear in the original text as it helps create an air of anonymity for the characters while keeping a crisp and breezy flow. I like to think that this is as close as you'll get to the original Spanish version. I also like to think of myself as a traditional "3" but I'll let others be the judge of that. To Facundo, *gracias pibe, a sido todo un honor ser parte del equipo*. Enjoy.

# JUEGO DE CHICOS

INTRODUCTION

1

# INDEX

## <<TURQUESA>>

**1**

What a tumult there was the day that "Turquesa" first appeared! At first, it seemed cool and we kind of liked having a tranny on our team, it gave our team of "gay machos" a little glamour. Later, after we saw her juggle the ball, all of us were saying pretty much the same thing:

—She plays better than we do, what a bitch!

But that wasn't the problem. We trained once, twice, three times with her; or more accurately, she trained us, and it was all good. Until a player complained because his back was shredded by her fingernails. After, "5" did it as well and later still "7:"

—It's just that "Turquesa" had long nails, sharp and pointy, like a witch's —he said, drying the blood that dripped off his back. He forgot to add that her nails were also dirty on the inside and unpainted.

Other afternoons I was surprised to walk with her until the end of the property. "Turquesa" talked and I listened to her. She told me she was from Jujuy and that she hadn't been in Buenos Aires for too long. In her province she had nine brothers, except one that was a cop who came with her. She got around on a motorcycle to explore the city. The lodge where she lived was in San Telmo. She worked as a prostitute in an adult movie theater in Congreso. The majority of her clients were married men, according to her, because their rings shone in the darkness; but they were sexually passive.

—It gets boring sucking cocks, what I really like is to get fucked —she told me in a hoarse voice, her village accent thick, like someone you find that you can tell everything to, without shame or feeling you'll get judged.

When she arrived and dismounted, her high heels would stick in the mud. We had to help her, grabbing her by the arm while she grabbed ours to unstick her. After, she would change and put on her silvery cleats. A couple of times she tripped over a rock and bitched and moaned about it for a while. Sometimes, when she would take off on her motorcycle, the helmet would fall off and she would have to come back to get it.

She was in a state-funded treatment, assisted by a cadre of psychologists, psychiatrists, and doctors, that helped her with her issue. It wasn't difficult for her to tell me she was going through the process and becoming "trans." Cutting off one's cock to get a pussy, I repeated to myself. To my surprise, she reveled to me that sexually, the best time she had ever had, had been with a chick. She added:

—There's nothing like lesbians... I am positive that if I get an operation, I will turn lesbian —I didn't know if she was talking to me seriously or completely taking the piss. Let's review: a transvestite with the name of the color that identifies boys, intends to play football on a team of mostly gay men. She introduces herself saying that she is a woman, but she has male genitals and says that she will get an operation to make herself transsexual; and lesbian.

After drinking some water under the sun, I understood that it wasn't all black and white, and that sexual diversity goes farther than just being a man, woman, homosexual, bisexual, tri-sexual; there's something for everyone and for all the tastes…

The problem arose after a match in Parque Sarmiento, where she got close to Coach and asked him in front of everyone why he made her go to the scrimmages and didn't play her in official games. Screaming and pointing her index finger everywhere, she demanded a response. The Boca jersey was crushing her tits. An administrator tried to explain to her that the commission's intention was to protect her, that they couldn't play her in tournaments that by regulation were for men. Because she was a transvestite, that wanted to be a woman, it was impossible for her to play. A guy on the team, before Coach's silence, said it was because of her breasts.

—Tits, kid, she corrected him, exalted, but not in a sexy way.
—We're scared that something is going to happen to them.
—Them? Who?

—Your tits, dumb ass. We're trying to protect you he said to her.

—She's not Coca Sarli —said "6." But this time there were only a few that didn't laugh. This was serious.

—What do we do if they elbow you in the tits? And, with the whole thing about medical coverage? —said "7."

This had gotten out of hand. We were carrying our bags on our shoulders, ready to leave to go home, but the situation made us re-huddle. We took off our bags, left them under a tree and circled-up an improvised meeting.

—Hey, what the fuck are we going to do with "Turquesa?" She's not bad, but... you think she's worth us fighting for her? —I heard "2" say a week before the blowout. The question traveled for days over our emails and text messages. Now the problem stopped being in our cells, but to be decided on the pitch. We passed ourselves the question like it were the ball but without pressing to midfield and without anybody taking a shot on goal.

The Captain of the team said what we were all thinking:

—This is a team of gay men, about 80 or 90 percent gay. We demand our place in society. Our place as men, beyond gay or not gay. We don't want to be identified as harpies... we can pick a boy or a man to love, or for a quickie, but after... we have the same pains, anxieties, pleasures and rights as any other person. We don't want any more discrimination, no. What we want is to occupy a place in society like any other person...

—Bah! That's not the point! —interrupted "7."

—Aside from our sexual preference, why can't we play football, man to man, with heterosexual people? —at that moment there was a murmur heard that grew in intensity and began to loop repetitively:

—Don't discriminate... don't discriminate...! —we jeered as if we were taking a political action or in the bleachers shouting for our favorite team. The words came out accompanied by drumming on whatever was near: a branch from a tree, a gym bag, "Turquesa's" motorcycle, the stone where we sat...

—Why has an imagined social norm sprung up over another? As if one way were bad and the other way were good. Who should be able to determine if one game is exclusively for heteros and another for gays? Ah? Who? Most of those of us here are gay and we like it… —continued the Captain.

—Dick and ass —someone said.

—Playing ball. What's the problem?

Those words of solidarity were interrupted by the Captain who continued with his discourse:

—Labeling gay people, outside of the line that says gays can and can't do this…

"Sub 10" chimed in:

—In other words, you want to show that you can be gay and macho at the same time… It doesn't strike me as an affront to the system… not change… what you're doing is gay militancy and if you want to sell the image of "gay machos" so that more repressed people sign up just so you can say, I have a million followers… I would have to resign… I'd resign.

—No… no… —screamed a kid in the back that was covered by others, not letting him talk.

"Sub 10," who had only recently incorporated himself into the team, kept saying:

—What's the problem here? You don't want "Turquesa" because she's a tranny? And you guys are always talking about being discriminated against?

A group of three kids that seemed like they didn't give a fuck about anything, that seemed like they were getting a rise from the situation, began again to beat their gym bags and to jeer as if they were at a game, like they had just done it, and more than one time managed to pull off: in a public bus, in the subway, at a restaurant:

—Don't discriminate… don't discriminate… don't discriminate…

The look on Coach's face was severe. It produced a silence which nobody could fill. After a while, we heard a calmer voice, that proved there were signs of wanting to return and open a dialogue.

—Discriminating is not accepting everything —and kept talking while someone interrupted him, and then another person interrupted that one and started talking and no one was hearing what was being said. When we realized what was happening, we shut up out of shame and began again to listen to the person that was talking.

—To discriminate is to be able to choose with whom one will play. If everyone plays then how are we different, so it doesn't make much sense that everyone should play... one decides. Life is like that. Consciously or unconsciously we are always making decisions, discriminating between one thing and another. If your problem is with the word: discriminate, well then, I say we use the word: discern.

—And? What will that prove? —said "Sub 10" this time more agitated, almost screaming.

—What will it prove? Let's see... what sense is there playing with a masculine pose? Also, if you guys are so courageous as to leave "Turquesa" out, why didn't y'all have the balls when she approached us at the club in San Telmo and asked us to play? There no one said shit, right? I don't understand. There no one said nothing, huh? I don't understannnnnnnnnnnnnd... Why didn't you say anything if that is not what you wanted?

—Okay, if she wants to play, she can do that, but we want her to bring a certificate signed by a notary about playing with men is purely her responsibility just in case something happens so we can be clear of any liability...

—No, if she has to come with a certificate then I am opposed. Then, we should all have to come with certificates from our doctors. It's semi ridiculous what you're proposing, dude.

—No, it's just that if something happens to her it's different. She has breasts, she's a woman...

—Why? Why? She has a body like everyone else... a body is a body, regardless of differences in gender. A bo-dy. Who doesn't have a body? Now... if we that are gay and play with gay people and we get together for barbecues or go dancing, because we definitely get together to enjoy things we can't with others... because football is a social activity, an act of integration... and if we get together with other gay people it's because at some point they discriminated against us... I don't know why we feel we have to do the same with "Turquesa." Because she's a tranny and future transsexual? Now, if we that are gay are going to start to discriminate between ourselves... I don't know...

—No. It's different... because she's a tranny, a transsexual, it's not the same as being gay. Her gay is different... she says she's a woman... a woman... understand?

—And? And, what? We're going to discriminate against her because she's a woman... with that criteria let's discriminate against the passive ones from the less passive ones, and the ones that take the whole dick versus those that only eat the tip, and the ones who only suck it... I don't know... I don't understand anything anymore. I don't know where I'm at, where I've taken heed of myself... you guys are more judgy than my mother...

—No "Sub 10," this is an open group formed 11 years ago, but with definitions, with parameters, with limits. It was determined and defined that you could be like you wanted, always, whether you're straight or gay... Transvestites, women, and trans-women can form their own team. We want to play against teams of men that will accept us is, beyond our own sexual condition, understand? If we leave "Turquesa" in this, we are giving a motivation for them to keep seeing us as...

—How? How? Like what? C'mon and say it, like man-whores, like whores, like unrepentant doodads, if that's what we are and if not, take a look at yourself.

The discussion had wandered into unchartered territory.

—In my opinion, they discriminate. I mean to say, we're discriminating —I said carefully.

—You don't understand that we don't have the conditions for a transvestite to play on the team. The team is gay with some heterosexuals. This is the formula for our team —said the Captain, screaming, emphasizing every word. He paused for some air and said:

—During the first conference we traveled to, only two of the heteros participated because the rule was no more than two. Why? Cuz basically: We. Are. A. Gay. Team. Why is it I have to explain this?

—Who makes the rules?

—The international association... the dykes can form a team with trannies... it's not that complicated... they can put an ad on the Internet and summon people like we did... Don't forget we started out with two people and now look at everything we've become. We are easily more than 30.

—Talking about this now... you know what the problem is?

—We didn't prohibit "Turquesa" to come and play... we are the least indicated to discriminate. But it's been ten years that we played the same way. She's starting a problem, plain and simple.

—Whoever told her to come without telling her that she wouldn't be able to play in the games against other "hetero" teams, didn't tell her this and now...

—Yeah, it's true... They should've told her it was a gay team, and not a tranny one... nobody stepped up to tell her what's what, that much is true.

—We don't want anybody to feel bad.

—It's not that simple... Look at Coach, he hasn't been able to get a word in at all.

—Yes, and you still have not agreed on several points —said "Sub 10" again.

—Guys... let's leave this for Tuesday —said Coach.

—We don't discriminate... we decided... we accept some things and others no... we intend to abide by the regulations like in '99 and '03. —We've dealt with this before, we've already lived this situation but I feel it was resolved... that transvestite put a team together with lesbians... this is a gay team. So, then, what you are saying is, come here but don't come in.

—It's just that at Cantillo, for example, she won't be able to play... and in the Gay World Cup, either, so what's the point?

The guys began to disperse. Some leaned up against a tree. One came down from the canopy from where he was watching the discussion, another one let go the branch he had been hanging from. Someone passed around a bottle of sparkling water that had been thawing. We all drank from the same lip. The bottle made its way to "Turquesa," but she turned it down. At that time of the afternoon, after having played two intense games against the heteros, we were more than tired: we had exploded. The sun was strong and even words hurt our heads like razors.

—We're not discriminating... we are choosing... one chooses their own paths.

—...

—Please use the same criteria for everything, dumbass.

—You guys are letting me down... What is the common read on this situation? For example, for my grandmother, two dudes going down on each other, from her point of view, is an abomination, and both dudes would be diagnosed as abnormal by her.

—It's not the same thing to be a transvestite than it is to be gay.

—What? The way in which people dress determines what people are? Is that right?

—And... I repeat, it is NOT the same thing to be a transvestite than it is to be gay.

—You guys are really letting me down.

The guys left under the tree began to talk amongst themselves.

—Is this a football team that is gay, gay, gay? What is it for you to be gay? Gay... a gay team. Not comprised of lesbians... nor transvestites, or clowns.

—The problem is yours since you don't understand that here there are rules and definitions, regulations.

—The trannies are looking to become women... male genitals bother them; they consider themselves to be transgender... If she says that she wants to be a woman, then she should go get an operation... she wants us to consider her a woman, but then she comes and plays with men, in a football derby saying she's a woman... I don't know... I don't get any of it... it's very strange.

—In my grandmother's eyes, a guy that sucks another guy is also very strange.

—You already said that.

—Okay... I'll wait for you guys on Tuesday... and very well what you did today —said Coach to close the discussion.

Someone said:

—Let's go because "Turquesa's" already growing a beard...

She grabbed her things, sat on a rock and untied her cleats. She took off the tape from her ankles, the same tape that protects her tits and walked alone to the street, just as she had when she arrived. "Sub 10" left through the opposite exit, also alone.

**2**

After that Sunday, "Turquesa" disappeared. She didn't call us back, like she used to before practices to confirm time and place. Because she didn't use Facebook, we decided to call her cell. We left a message. The guys were mad that she might report us to INADI. She never answered. We lost her trail after six months.

At the end of last year, she appeared at one of our trainings. We figured someone must have called her to tell her where we would be training. From the first moment, she said she knew it wasn't possible for her to play in championships and that she didn't care about that, that she had read the regulations and that we were right, that she had to find a team of lesbians, transvestites, or transgender people, but until now she hadn't found it, she thought of coming to watch us play, that is if we let her. She brought *mate* and some biscuits.

She began going to all the trainings. Every time she came, "6" greeted her with a hug before she got off her motorcycle. He looked at her with admiration. I sang her part of The Cure's "Why Can't I Be You" and "6" laughed. One day she asked her for her footballing skills. He hoisted her off the grass and they spun in circles like Wonder Woman. That day, while we played, "Turquesa" hyped us up as if she were on the pitch. On another day, seated under a tree, she told us about the time she sucked a cop's cock for three hours, in Jujuy, and had to sit on the stick shift to cum. We burst laughing. We wanted to hear more of her stories; she had a bunch to tell. At San Telmo, the keeper had to leave because he was literally shitting his pants. The sun was coming in through the highway median, inundating the field with light. She came closer to where we were fucking around and told us that one night she was working the highway with a friend. Her friend, "La Choclo," needed to take a shit so she went to the bushes. But, there was a girl already in the bushes sucking dick, and that girl came back spooked. Girlfriend, girlfriend, you aborted (because she had been walking around saying she'd gotten pregnant). No, we didn't abort, "Turquesa" told the girl, and the girl replied, but look, look at its hands, its eyes. No, dumbass, the girl that had gone to shit told her, there's a frog under that turd. And she returned to work the highway, rubbing her stomach.

Another day she came by with a Tupperware. She had some tamales that a sister had sent her through the mail. With a knife, she cut the tamales into bits so we could all share. While we stretched and put on our cleats, she told us that she had a date for her procedure to cut off her penis and make the gender-switch official with the government. She added that everything was going as planned. I kept seeing her alone, and confirmed my suspicions when I asked her about it. She kept living at the lodge in San Telmo, but without her brother who'd moved in with his girlfriend. We told her everything was cool, that she could train with us only if she cut her nails (they were still long, sharp, and dirty).

3

"Turquesa" trained when she could. She worked at night and slept during the day which left her very little time. On top of that, because of the hormone treatments, she had to follow a strict schedule of weekly doctor visits. We weren't sure why but she didn't hold a grudge against us. She was always tender towards us. She says that she always felt like part of the team, even before meeting us. And it is true, she looks very comfortable around us. Now, some of the guys on the team like to be with her.

4

Last week was the most important day in her life. According to
"Turquesa:" her real birth. She wasn't alone in the hospital room. A
couple of guys from the team went to see her. We brought her a signed
jersey and a Boca pennant that she hung above the bed. She took pictures
with us. We uploaded them to Facebook. In the pictures, we're touching
her hair, sticking out our tongues, giving a nice "fuck you" to the
camera, all of us kissing her at once. We promised to title the album,
"Bedding Turquesa." But more than Madonna, she looked like a girl,
that would've liked to be a boy, just to play with us in the park until the
night was well, well under way.

<<1>>
## FOSFORITO

At night, after training and surrounded by a pesky cloud of mosquitoes, Fosforito, the team's goalie, announced he was leaving the team. Citing the school's schedule and his long commute from La Plata, he declared it an impossibility to continue coming to the capital. Suddenly, he insisted that "7" celebrated his upcoming birthday which was weird because he'd never been too keen on partying with the group. After much insistence and caving into Fosforito's awkward pressure, he agreed.

Two weeks later, on a Friday night, we met up at "7's" apartment; Fosforito had been the first to arrive. I sat next to him and while I chewed on a pink gum stick, he pressed me with questions about the guys on the team who hadn't arrived yet. "9" had plastic plates and was arranging a small mountain of diced ham and cheeses on them. "7" was busy reheating the *pizzettas* his *nonna* had made. "10" was on a roll, cracking joke after joke—even if no one was laughing at them. The new Depeche Mode album spun almost quietly in the background. We waited for "8's" show, drinking beers and Coca-Cola, eating French fries and sausages. The buzzer rang and Fosforito went downstairs to open the door. "8" was still in "7's" room trying on wigs. I walked in without knocking and saw him; he was naked, putting on makeup like Robert Smith. He was going to lip-synch Isabel Pantoja or Valeria Lynch—it didn't matter; he didn't know any of their lyrics. "Don't say anything," he said laughing. I returned to the living room as two dudes dressed in black kicked their way in. They had balaclavas on, their eyes almost imperceptible through the holes. One was armed. With the gun held high, he ran towards the table, knocking over glasses. A beer bottle rolled off and smashed on the floor. My heart was in my throat.

Everyone against the wall. Move it now! –said the one with him.
—Now lower your pants –he ordered.

The silhouettes of our soccer team automatically projected onto the wall. An invisible hand had turned the music off and the silence cut the air. They took off their t-shirts. Turning my head, I could see the one with the gun putting on a cap as a Sex Pistols tune remixed with rap began to play. The men in black started breakdancing in a way that I couldn't believe. One dropped his head to the floor and spun like a top. Still shaken and in shock we saw them pull their large dicks out, pointing them menacingly towards the apartment's owner. One started jacking off with exaggerated fanfare. At the height of it, before he climaxed, he tucked it away, raised his hand in a mock Isabelita hello wave; and like that they were gone. A mix of excitement and fear hung in the air. Low voices rumbled amongst the small group; some said they knew it had been a joke though their faces remained pale.

—It all happened very fast, but intense —said the team doctor. There was a before and after to that episode. When "2" put on the Ramones, I returned to sit next to Fosforito. Drinking beer after beer, he told me that that had been his birthday gift. Without thinking I looked into his eyes and asked what his real reason for leaving was. After considering for what felt like an eternity, he whispered into my ear:

—Don't tell anyone, but Juan Vucetich got into the school. I want to be a cop. –That last statement carrying the gravity to slay my doubts about what he had said.

—I passed the exams –he burped, thick with the smell of mustard—. You need to board for the school… whenever I get a free weekend and I can get out, I'll call you so we can get a pickup game going with the boys…

At that moment, "8" made his entrance. He looked like shit. Since "7" didn't have any dresses or skirts, he had put on a tablecloth around his waist which did little to cover his muscular and hairy legs. His makeup, done up with markers, was awful. He was sweating profusely and it was turning it into a runny patch of oil that gave him an air of Alice Cooper. The pink wig "7" had saved from a *carioca* carnival kept falling with his moves. "8" ran around, jumping on top of us; everyone agape, receiving him like a torpedo. His lips went one way and the lyrics another: "More… every day you give me more," was all we could hear over Valeria Lynch's voice. That was his birthday gift.

Fosforito got up, started dancing on a chair, his eyes closed. The guys catcalled him: "Madonna is a manly man next to you…," "What a woman!" "Baaaay-beeee, you know it!" The goalie loved it; loved being called Miss Fosforito. As he danced, he transformed into another person.

Two days ago, I walked into a Chinese market on Corrientes. I was surprised to see a thick pair of legs snugged into slacks in front of the cashier. The package forced into them bulged with brazen defiance. I looked up to find a policeman's uniform. After our gazes met, we embraced. Fosforito told me he had been patrolling this beat. He leaned into me and whispered into my ear like he had that time when he told me he wanted to be a cop, that he was fucking now more than ever. It was his turn to pay. He hugged me again before getting into the squad car out on the street. I think he put the siren on to show off, so I'd sit there, thinking about him; or her, like he liked being called.

## <<SUB 2>>
## LA BUDA

"3's" laptop has a slideshow of team photos: the barbecues, the bus rides with our kits, playing on different pitches, birthday parties; some in the locker-rooms, like the one of "Sub 2" who's laughing at the camera, like Spongebob Squarepants.

It's been more than two months and he still can't believe it, he can't make any sense out of it. He stopped doing what he liked best: dancing and meeting cuties. He's missing practices too. I think he's gonna leave the team. There's a "3" before and after the episode. This affected us all, but not as much as it affected him. All he does is stare at the photos now.

Less than a week before the match at Entre Ríos, we trained in Buenos Aires filled with an unusual sense of excitement and joy, regardless of the daylong trip ahead of us. The jokes and laughter ebbed and flowed all day. "Sub 7" proposed a quick round of "Passive/Aggressive" takeaway for warmups. Some agreed, some told him to fuck off. When someone didn't pass the ball, they got catcalled: "c'mon passive passive, passssssssssive." "10" and "9" picked the starting 11, instead of odds and evens, they said cocks and asses.

That game was a disaster. It was a landslide of goals. "Turquesa" challenged "Sub 2" with a hard elbow that left him bleeding and out of the match. Something similar happened to "Sub 7." We missed eight shots, and the one we got didn't really count for us since the keeper got a hand on it and it spun out of his grip into the goal.

—What you got in them hands fatso? Butter? —yelled one of the guys on his team. The keeper didn't miss a beat:

—Cum, you fuck. But not yours... —we all laughed. It didn't escalate from there.

Regardless of the goal difference that day, we were sure we'd win the derby. "Sub 2" or "La Buda" like we teased to get a reaction from him, played very well—quiet though. When he entered the pitch, he had an air of mysticism.

The teams shared lockers that afternoon, which was nice since we rarely had access to one on away games. We usually changed behind one of the goals. In the past, we usually ignored them if they were provided. The bulk of the team waited outside because they didn't like showering in front of others. Some showered in their briefs and some held a washcloth over their privates. "4" would dry his back, telling the same old jokes. "La Buda" would sit in quiet meditation on a bench. He was the only one who didn't laugh. He didn't really interact with the team, except for "3." Specially after training, when they'd exchange a couple of words and a few glances. No one else picked up on that.

That Friday, the team, got together outside River's stadium, waiting for the bus for the long trip. "3" was the only who noticed "La Buda" wasn't there and remarked immediately:

—Where is he? He didn't come.

After a minute, he added, knowingly:

—He's not coming.

Nobody paid him any mind. Before we boarded, Coach asked us into the station's cafeteria. We usually shared a sense of excitement when we got together. This time it was different, maybe because we weren't all together. Coach was having problems talking. He stuttered. Started sentences that went nowhere. He'd bite his lips, roll his eyes, and kept shifting his weight on his feet from side to side. Finally, he looked at the clock and let it all out:

—Boys, in Entre Ríos we have to play… and we have to win. For you, for us, and for, for, for… "Sub 2." Because "Sub 2…" Because "Sub 2's" not coming.

From the back of the cafeteria we heard:

—We know, he got hemmed-up in someone's bed like a dog—…

Nobody laughed, like we already knew what he was about to say.

—He didn't quit the team… he quit life –and there he broke down, sobbing for a few seconds. Once he found his bearings and composed himself a bit, he said:

—We have to do it –his words bouncing around the room like an echo until they fell on us. His words looped in my mind.

"3's" still looking at the photos, looking to see if he can see some kind of message in the eyes of "La Buda." He's looking for something through the screen, in the memories of the few words they shared, or the last time he said hi, or the time he was on his way to his house and said:

—Later tiger, I'll see you tomorrow –as he turned to check him out a couple of times as he walked away. Now "3's" saying La Buda used to communicate with him telepathically.

We got back in time for the wake but we couldn't say our goodbyes. "9" wanted to know why; he was screaming through the door wanting to know why we couldn't come in. The mother came out, visibly upset, talking into the wind and looking towards the heavens:

—It was an accident… an accident, Julián was cleaning his father's gun…

The few of us who stayed behind had to cross the street by order of the grieving family. A little later, since we weren't leaving, the rent-a-cop they had at the funeral home kicked us out. Right before sunrise, at the bus stop, "3" told us:

—I can't stop thinking about all the things "La Buda" told me without speaking. He believed that I understood him, that I knew everything about him, that I'd save him, but I was too late. Why didn't I do something? I knew that was going to happen.

<<3>>

## WORMS CRAWLED THROUGH HIS TEETH

The first time I laid eyes on "3" he seemed like he was from outer space, like he had traveled a long time to make it to the scrimmage. He looked like a mix of "Wally Gator" and "Penelope Pitstop." He landed tired, his arms limp to his sides, dragging his feet. He was searching for destiny, letting himself be led intuitively. When he looked at the pitch he saw us and thought he recognized us. At first, he didn't join the team, but as time went by, he got closer and closer with the guys and more familiar, until he reached the apex of faggotry. One day he started talking like Granny Gasalla, and then another day like a full broad. Whenever anybody had a good play, or scored, "3" would shout: "Well done my queen!" "Goddess," "My beauty," "Divine." Some laughed, some didn't care, very few played along. "3" liked to change the names of things: boots became "spikes," the ball "cock," the guys "bums," boyfriends "hubbies," the list went on and on... In any case, aside from being a little jarring, we took him in immediately.

"3" saw himself as a defender, but, those who know football and understand the game, will say that it was the first time he set a foot on a pitch. One afternoon, the team captain threw a pair of gloves at him and told him to takeover at goal. He called it "the jogging spot." In little time we started noticing some changes. "3" wasn't a good goalie, but he worked hard at it, putting in extra effort. In a few weeks' time, he was already saving better. The majority of the goals we got on him, according to Coach, were due to the strength of the strikes.

—A bit of object fright —added the Physical Trainer —"3" has good focusing and an admirable sense of precision —he continued.

—Doesn't miss any practice. He's punctual and —added Coach.

—He takes it seriously... That's true. I like that he lunges into the ball, faces strikers to shorten angles and dives, like a cat, right? —said the Physical Trainer.

—Yes. And he stays down after a save, looking at you with beady eyes like a rat... —it went quiet. Coach reflected on something and then spoke so as to further define the thought:

—The fucker moves like a rolling pin, he goes back and forth with the ball, he looks like he's making a pizza, like my witch wife who spends all day rolling dough. And, another thing the guy's got: he always wears the team jersey. Sometimes Banfield's, which we'll have to burn, but whatever... —said Coach semiseriously at a barbecue, while giving a little feedback on each one of us. "3" kept tossing the salads and listening intently to what was said of him, he kept his happiness to himself, smiling into the lettuce bowl.

To the team's great surprise, "3" was up-to-date and informed on matches from the A, B, and C lower divisions. He was learning about goal scorers and European clubs like Real Madrid and Liverpool. He read the sports pages of every newspaper like it was a textbook he had to study; like a test was coming up. You could tell he wanted to be a part of the team and win a spot in it.

He lived in Florencio Varela. To practice, he'd walk eight blocks from his house to the 145 stop. Then he'd take a train to Constitución. From what he'd say, he'd kill time going into the restroom to look at cocks with one eye on the clock. He'd then connect on a jitney to Palermo, where we trained.

When he laughed, it looked like worms crawled through his teeth. He was 33, but we thought him older than that. He worked in a warehouse sorting garbage. He'd graduated with a law degree a few years before but never practiced. He had also studied English. He'd download gay-themed movies online. If they weren't dubbed, he'd dub them himself with whatever proficiency he had with the language.

He lived with his folks. They were elderly and had come from Corrientes when they were young, looking for a brighter economic future they never found. A little after joining the team, "3's" mom found his team card while cleaning his room. It had the rainbow flag on it, and just in case there were any doubts, it said "Gay Footballers" underneath and "3's" full name. He couldn't deny anything. His mom, a few days before, had gone into his room to bring him a steak and salad on a tray.

She found him in bed, watching two naked guys kissing in prison. He told her then, luckily, that it wasn't what she thought, it was an unforeseen development in the plot of the movie he was watching. But now he had no other option but to face it and tell her the truth of who he was and what he was doing.

She reacted with a barrage of insults. Leaving and slamming the door. She kept screaming from the other side of the closed door. Saying she'd kill herself if he didn't change. "3" held his own: "I've been, am and will be gay, mom" he shouted back. At night, he tried explaining the same to his old man, a man of advanced age and few words, who still worked construction jobs. His mom had already called him on his cell and told him before he left work; amidst cries, anger and concerns. He reacted to this by disowning him and kicking him out of the house.

"3" spent four months slumming in a teammate's apartment. He didn't have any gay friends then. He'd led a closeted life, even had a girlfriend over in the Susana neighborhood. She was a hairdresser and friends with his mom. They'd drink afternoon *mates* together.

After practice, when it was dark out, he'd put on a pair of skinny imitation Adidas sweats he'd bought at the street market, and get lost among Palermo's trees. We'd see him walk around like a crazy person, without memory, driven by an unseen superior force that was dragging him through the forest. His legs and feet moved independently, looking for a man, like a magnet attracting metal. Intuition would take him to where the guys were waiting, like wolves in heat. When a man would see him from afar, "3" would get close so they could take a better look at him. Once he had their attention, he'd pretend to take a piss on a tree while the john got closer, slowly, he'd undo his pants revealing his ass. There were nights he'd walk through the trees, for hours, without hooking anyone with this game. He told me that one night he came across two lights in the dead of dark. They froze him. It was a cat, hidden deep in the brush. He became transfixed, couldn't take a step, until he felt the bulge of someone pushing up against him. When he turned to look, he was confronted with the face of a woman that wasn't. "3" told me his scream left the forest deaf. It was like looking in a mirror, that man's face made-up to look like a broad. He bolted. From that day on he stopped talking like a woman. He understood then, that he didn't have to go through that in order to hook up with a guy.

The time he lived away from his parents allowed him to see things for what they were, and that he had fallen into a game of roles: the "macho" guy at home in front of his parents and a "broad" on the streets or at practice. Before, he'd maintain sexual relations without investing affection. Most of the time he just slept with "bums." The pleasure of a naked, anonymous body excited him beyond control. After, he'd return to the solace and solitude of trains and his garbage warehouse. He was thinking that now, he'd try a real relationship for the first time, he told us one afternoon, and started asking about places where he could meet guys with his same interests.

One morning, his dad called to tell him there was a parcel for him to pick up. He returned to his folks' home, with a clear conscience and a plan, ready to start life anew. "This time I'll go step by step," he told me, happy. He was seeing a psychologist, of which he said he had fallen in love with. "He's a god, a god," he'd parrot over and over when he talked about him.

He was trying really hard for his spot on the team. At the last meeting, Coach called him up and told him he could return to the defense as the "3," the position of his dreams. The other day he told us:

—I want to fulfill all of my dreams and shed the past —he seemed determined. I believed him, so did many of the guys.

—You can count on us dude —said "11."

Last night I got a text from "4" which said he'd seen him hanging in the trees of Palermo, his ass out, showing it off to the homeless guys there. What the guys don't know yet, is the text I got from "3:" "For the first time in my life, Facu, I'm happy. I'll worry about tomorrow, tomorrow." Ramón, the guy who lights the oil can fires at the park when it gets cold and El Santiagueño, who's always looking for food in the trash, are his boyfriends.

*We played under the expressway. Rain was coming in sideways, drenching the pitch. The thunder and lightning was nonstop. We started at eight o'clock. When we were about to finish, closer to 11, it was still raining with the same intensity from earlier. We played until midnight that time. We left and it was still raining. We had pizza and empanadas with ice cold Cokes at "La Furia." The whole team agreed; we'd never seen rain like that, and in that way...*

## <<4>>
## COWS THROUGH THE WINDOW

### 1

"4" just turned 31. He's stout, thick, hairy. We call him "teddy bear." He works as a personal trainer. Seeing his colleagues at the gym in the showers doesn't even move a hair on him. He's never been with a guy his age. He's not interested. He gets hot for grandpas.

When our physiotherapist can't make it to practice, "4" takes point and leads our runs: from the Güemes Monument down to River. Afterwards, he runs a circuit with the orange cones that glow in the dark. We do his stretches when we're done. He shares everything with us: water, cereal bars, bananas (which are mandatory because they reenergize muscles and some of us always forget to bring). After training, "4" gives lifts to some of the guys in his car. Ataque 77, two David Bowie songs, one Ramones, and Soda Stereo blaring from the speakers. The disc looping after it ends. Every Tuesday we hear the same music. Ever since the night "7" interrupted the Ramones' "Baby I Love You" to put on the Rock & Pop radio station, the stereo mysteriously stopped working.

### 2

—Did I tell you Wenceslao doesn't want to see me again? He says I'm too young for him, that he's got strong feelings for me, and that in the end, I'm gonna leave him for another guy... someone younger. He's crazy! Wenceslao is stubborn, hard as marble, he doesn't get it that I want to be with him, that I like older guys. The older the better, but he doesn't get it –says "4" as he brakes his Peugeot 206 to a stop at the corner. The light turns red and momentarily stops the narrative. We both feel the silence, each other's presence. We haven't showered and we're tired from the scrimmage. Our eyes wander to the restaurant across the street. We see skirt steaks, chicken and a strip loin on the grill. The table ramekins overflow with creole sauce. The car starts again and "4" tells me of a great play the new guy made.

—He's talented... plays well..., Wenceslao doesn't want to see me again. He called to tell me we shouldn't see each other, because I'm gonna leave him one of these days... so... I'm single again. You have no idea how sad it is to cook dinner alone, eat alone, sleep alone...

—I get it, my friend –I tell him, though I feel like he's not listening so I continue– I live alone too.

—I'll take you home.

—No man, it's cool, I can get off here and walk. It's only five blocks away anyways.

—No, no... I'll take you home... Ah! I have to tell you: Wenceslao doesn't want to see me anymore. He called to tell me I'm too young, that he's twice my age, that he can't be with me because in the end, I'm gonna leave him...


**3**


One night, in New York, after our World Cup, I went with "4" to the "Down Town Bar." I think it's the swankiest spot in Manhattan where all the old moneyed sluts get together. Suit and tie was mandatory attire. The majority of them wore white blazers with silk pastel ties. You could see a grand piano from the door. A woman, holding a goblet of brandy was singing jazz standards. The rough median age was 70. "4" was excited, not from the games we had played the prior week, but from the throng of grandpas he kept greeting as they entered the joint like he was the party's host or was waiting for someone in particular. He told me that night, close to thirty times: "this one Facu, I'm marrying this one." Bored, I sat on a Le Corbusier chaise with a little Evian bottle that "4" had ponied up $20 for. As I finished the bottle and yawned, I thought about leaving and heading to the home we were staying at. "4" couldn't take his eyes off the geezer who was next to me. The man looked lonely. He made quite a show of getting up with a diamond-encrusted cane he'd kept hidden to the side of the couch. When he came back from the bathroom, "4" squared in front of him. They communicated awkwardly; the old man didn't speak Spanish and "4's" English was unsure. He turned out to be the owner of a chain of gas stations in Memphis. He was married. Had three boys who'd given him six grandkids. The geezer fell in love immediately but my friend changed his mind instantly. "4" fell in and out of love with the speed of an e-mail, a text message or a toilet's flush. "4" has spent his whole life looking for the "perfect older gentleman;" a man that never materialized. While I saw him like this, I remembered his father: a man in his seventies, who had died five years ago, just as he and "4" were getting to really know each other after he'd come out. I thought my friend would be alone his whole life. I asked myself if this is what he liked, what he wanted. "Piss them Facu. I love giving them golden showers…"

## 4

—I didn't tell you… the old man's owner of gas station chain in Memphis and…

—Yeah, you told me…

—Ah! But I didn't tell you he's got six grandsons…

I don't know why I did it, but I told him the secret. We had agreed we wouldn't tell "4" the latest on "El Paragua" (our sub or utility player), so he wouldn't get upset. Maybe it was the early morning cab ride we shared in New York or how far away we were from home that woke the desire to get that story off of my chest. "El Paragua," who also liked older guys, had met an eighty-year-old Venezuelan. The old guy had taken him back to his country. When he returned from Venezuela, he was greeted with the news that on the flight to Argentina, the old guy had croaked. The next day, he found out he had left him his entire inheritance. To him, "El Paragua!" A man who worked construction and odd jobs and didn't have a cent to pay for a jitney. It hadn't even been three months since they met and here he was, owner of a fortune. We never heard from him again.

## 5

—Did I tell you Wenceslao doesn't want to see me again? –"4" told me again while we rode a jitney to Entre Ríos. After a while, when the road curved and the orange groves appeared, he continued –He told me I'm too young, that he loves me a lot, and that in the end, I'm gonna leave him for another… someone, much younger than him –I was getting worried, hearing the same story over and over; I thought he might be going a bit crazy.

Could an old person inhabit a younger boy but retain the insistent ideas like a scratched CD? I thought of that and looked at him. He was falling asleep against the window. Outside, cows and pasture greeted us; there was nothing else. The worry left me as I realized though he was always repeating the same shit over and over, there was a wish in his words. He was looking for something and he would never find it: His dead father perhaps? It calmed me to think that "4" wasn't alone on this trip: I was with him and he was with me. I leaned into his shoulder and fell asleep. In that way we both forgot we were alone in this world. For a moment we were happy, like we were in our mother's womb. Until Coach blew his whistle and we had to deboard the bus and get on the pitch. Another battle, another game waited for us. At least we had dreamed a little bit, together.

## <<5>>
## THE GAME ON TV

"5" was without work and with a sick father. His old man had spent more than three years prostrate in bed, injecting himself with insulin. A couple of months ago, they cut off his leg, and later he became blind. From that moment on, the Coach told us, "5" has been running faster. And it was true, he would move his legs like a fan about to become discombobulated. For a while, it looked like he was running from someone or something, and would disappear. When I asked him why he was running like that, he told me: "Now, I know that death exists. I don't want to waste not one more moment. Legs are the most important thing." So, we nicknamed him "Roadrunner." In spite of having partial paralysis, hereditarily, he could move his left arm, but his right arm hung on his body, to his side, like a dried branch.

After a meeting with the Physical Trainer and Coach, they offered to change his position.

—From that moment on, he started playing more focused, with more force and precision —according to Coach.

—It looks like he found his place on this team —said "9" one night in-between beers at the disco we used to go to on Fridays.

—Now I live for the tea... football — (he wanted to say "team" but "football" is what came out) "5" told us with a sweaty water bottle in his hand.

During the game in "La Quemita," on the side of the Huracán field, "12" who shared a flat with "5" for a year and a half, asked me:

—You can't imagine the cock on him.

—And how did you see it? —I asked him as I sweat and copped a seat between him and "6" on the sub's bench.

—Have you seen his girlfriend...? Margot? —"12" asked me.

—Margarita, yeah.

—Okay, well, on Sundays when we would watch "Fútbol de Primera," they would send me out to buy beer and "5" would wink at me. I caught on to what was happening: dude's dick would get hard when the television came on for the game. "I'm nervous," he would say. But it was obvious... he would walk around the house with small shorts... imagine it! ... And that huge dong, moving from one side to another. At the beginning, when I came back from buying beer, I would ring the bell, even though I had the keys to the apartment. I used to notice that once I came in they would shift around on the couch. They used to also cover themselves with magazines, or a pillow. Then, I said to myself, it's my apartment. So, before going up, I was going to stop notifying them I'm coming up and I caught them. And not only once, but twice, three times I caught them... When "5" watched a game, he would make his chick suck it. How did he do it? I don't know. Not anyone can put their mouth around that whole bottle and she is so small... you see? But she didn't leave any of it out.

—Ha, ha, ha, ha.

—And you'd think when they saw me, the first time and the others, they'd stop doing it? They would be still for a second and then they would continue. She would move with more force, as if she wanted to rip it out at the root, that slut, and would eat it at the trunk. He had a super thick shaft, veiny. And, he'd push her head down, forcefully. The head of that bitch sank down to the shaft and disappear his cock.

—And you'd stay there, looking? —I asked "12" while we were sitting on the sub's bench, observing the plays in front of us. The other team was at our doorstep.

—No. I'd go straight to the kitchen, but I didn't miss a beat from my vantage point between dirty dishes and pots from the previous night. I will say one thing: they ain't coy. They knew I was looking, but they didn't say anything, they wouldn't stop, it only got worse.

—What an adrenaline rush!

—Imagine being so hot and bothered. "5" finished after a goal. She'd pound a glass of beer. I would walk across the living room and go to bed. Sometimes, I couldn't stand how hot they would get me and I would have to jerk off...

—Now I get why we called him the three-legged "Roadrunner" … ha, ha, ha...and without knowing it... pure intuition... or... did you christen him?"

—Nn. Naaaaah.

—And, he never had anything with someone on the team?

—Not that I know of. "5" is not gay. I don't think that he likes to fuck either. What excites him is watching footie and getting sucked off.

—I wonder if he gets hard when he's at the stadium?

At that moment, they called him into the game to play.

—I don't know... I'm going in... I'll be back.

"6" stayed sitting next to me. He had a tent in his pants. He had heard what "12" had told me. After a little while there was a free kick, but we weren't able to convert it. We kept losing two nil. The whistle blew and the game was over. In the dressing room I saw "6" close to "5." "5" didn't live with "12" anymore, he'd returned to his father's house. I learned from "3" that the living arrangement was unbearable. He would eat candy and cakes and all types of stuff his father couldn't eat in front of him. On top of that, the old man got homophobic again and he'd say homosexuals needed to be cured because they were sick; and that if they were allowed to marry, the next step would be to accept relationships between animals and men. "5" would try to make him reason, but it was impossible. When the conversation bordered on disrespect and insensitivity, "5" wanted to tell him that he deserved to be prostrate in bed, blind, with one leg, but he never got up the guts. After showering and getting dressed, as we were walking out, smelling of deodorant and wet hair, I heard "6" invite "5" to live with him.

—I have space, a lot of space —he said.

<<6>>
# DON'T TELL ANYONE

"6" told me the following story one Saturday afternoon when we were alone in the locker room after a match with Club Atlético de San Telmo. I promised I wouldn't tell anyone. He finished the story by the time we got to the corner kiosk where we downed a pair of Gatorades. Afterwards, I followed him to the metro station and was left alone with my thoughts...

Two weeks after moving in together, while they ate a homemade dinner, "5" told him he had dumped his girl and was now seeing Cantillo's ref, Marcela.

—The one with the two tails, nah, three –he specified and laughed. There was another one, a linesman but without tail – he laughed again. The next morning, while they drank *mates* before work, he asked him if he'd be cross if Marce spent the night. The sun had just snuck through the blinds, warming up the wooden floors. "6" walked over to a pot where his weed plant was beginning to show. He saw a little trail of ants. He squished them, one by one. He squirted hot water on the ones on the floor.

—No dude. This is our home now. You do whatever you want... but when I bring a dude over you ain't going to say shit, right?

"5" hugged him and left for work. "6" thought the day would never end. He was a shopping mall rent-a-cop. He spent all day longing for the night; making and revising plans in his head. Until he made a decision and was able to focus again on the shoppers coming in and out of the stores; their arms filled with packages and gifts.

When he got home, "6" didn't ring the bell. His heart was beating like a bomb ready to explode. He realized his mouth was dry and that if he had to speak, the words wouldn't come out. He opened a beer can and downed it in one gulp. He put the rest away, neatly, like they had been on the shelves of the Chinese market he'd bought them at.

Labels out. He walked down the hall to the living room. It was closed. He opened the door without knocking. He turned on the light. There was no one there. He went to "5's" room. He wasn't there. He went out to the corner store to get some produce. He hurried in case they were about to close. He bought eggplants, carrots and a dozen eggs. He prepped a vegetable lasagna. He cracked open another beer and lit a candle. He blew it out. He was afraid "5" would misunderstand and beat his ass. It was ten thirty and his friend wasn't home yet. After thinking it over, he called but it went straight to voicemail. He went to bed. He'd only eaten a small bit of cheese. He was restless, couldn't sleep, cocooning himself in the sheets nonstop; he looked like a cinnamon stick. "5" never showed up that night. Or the next day. He finally saw him during the Ezeiza training that Saturday morning. He made a big show of greeting everyone except him. He didn't talk to him all day, until finally, after training he said:

—You going home or what?

—Yeah dude, you? –asked "5."

—Yeah –said "6" tired, but happy about his friend's answer.

He sat next to him in the car and said:

—I wanna talk to you later dude, I got something rather important to tell you.

—No problem dude.

That night, "5" wasn't in the mood for lasagna. "6" ordered empanadas. He turned the TV off and started talking:

—Listen man, I'm nervous, about what I'm... I can't hold it, I gotta tell you. I thought it over a lot.

—Awright man, that's cool, go ahead...

—You sure? –asked "6."

—Yeah man. Talk... Who you kill? How much money you want? –and he laughed.

—Well, you know I... I've never been with a chick. And I'd like... I'd like for you to hook me up. I don't know, I wanna try. You know I like guys, a lot; they're the best. We are. But... I don't know? You? You've been... are with chicks... and... I don't know... it's a crazy idea I've had for a while and now, more than ever... I don't know if I'm explaining myself...

—Of course, how am I not gonna get that? Look, I only ended it with Marcela because the bitch was busting my balls. She just wanted to fuck all day and to be honest, I'd rather focus on the team... chick's horny as fuck. She likes it all. If you want, while we watch the Boca game, we can knock back a few beers and three-way her.

—Tag team?

—Yeah, but you're not fucking me because that'll ruin it.

—You're serious about this?

—Yeah. What's wrong? That ho's gonna like it so much and fuck you so good you'll never fuck another guy again. But whatever. If you still like dudes that's not my problem.

—Ah man! You have no idea how happy I am right now. I came and haven't even started...

—Ha ha. But you gotta behave. I'm gonna tell you one more time; you touch my dick while we're fucking her, and I will beat the living shit out of you. You hear? It's fucking over.

—I understand. You have my word. A gay man's word.

—Deal.

—Deal my friend.

They played again. When they got home, "5" phoned Marcela without showering. She got there in 20 minutes.

—I think she's horny –"5" said to his friend who was crippled by nerves and cramps in the bathroom, pretending to read a comic book— she's on her way.

The doorbell rang. "5" ran to the stereo to turn down the music. MGMT vanished. He opened the door for her. First thing he did was turn on the TV and put in a Boca DVD. He then opened a beer with his teeth. Marcela fidgeted in her seat, she looked bored. "5" wasn't feeling it. He diced a salami. He spread blue cheese on a piece of bread and sprinkled it with olives. He did the same with two other pieces of bread. He gave her one and ate another, leaving the third piece on the table. Marcela looked at him. "5" fast-forwarded the match, up to halftime. They were getting bored. The flush was heard and she asked him if there was anyone else there. "5" stuttered: yeah, no, yeah. His friend was vomiting in the bathroom. He came out, looking disheveled in his football shorts, his dick hard but it drooped almost immediately. Marcela wanted to leave. "6" was trembling. More than anything, "5" was sleepy. He tried touching her. He licked her thighs. She wasn't having it. "6" looked on from the hallway with a tray in hand thinking how ugly she was. He was trying to liken her to a bird; any bird, but couldn't think of one. He said to himself "women are the strangest thing there is" and went to his room. He went to sleep. He dreamt like he had never dreamt before. From that day on, there were no more birds in his dreams.

*On the trip to Uruguay, a digital camera disappeared from "12's" kit. We never found out who took it.*

<<7>>
## WEDDING SECRETS

A few days ago, while eating a cheese and salami sandwich at El Banderín, "7" told me about his chat with his best friend from Pigüé:

—One day I grabbed the dude and I told him straight up... I've been your friend since we were four years old and I dove right into it: Look here homie, I'm not seeing Lucía anymore and the dude tells me: "but if you're seeing her every night... then, who are you fucking?" I didn't skip a beat: "My girl's uh uh... Ariel, the handyman's son. There. I had to tell you. There it is and there's nothing more to it."

After thinking a moment, he said: "and me? What about me, wouldn't you want something with me, eh?" Nah, take it easy, you're not my type Coco. Nah, you don't turn me on. You're good looking and the chicks dig you man, and I admire you for that, but with you? Nah. After a few days, while shooting pool, the dude tells me he's gonna marry his girl. With the cue in hand, I yelled for the whole bar to hear that we'd be throwing his stag. He then whispered to me, that he'd rather stag with me, alone. What the fuck bit you? I asked and he told me, that he was serious, since I had been his unconditional friend his whole life. Every time we'd get together, we'd drink ourselves blind. Like a death wish. We couldn't say no, we'd even drink the water from a flower vase... the entire town's beer... and fucked up he told me: I'm marrying a girl I don't love. I yelled at him, what? Why're you doing this? If you're not sure Coco, don't do it... it's a few days away, you've got time. If you wanna get married, find one you love. You've got girls falling off of the rafters. No. I'm sure I want to get married, the dude tells me; the problem's I'm in love with another...

—Hold that, I gotta piss –I interrupted "7" while I pushed the stool to get up from the bar. I thought I could get my thoughts together in the pisser. I skimmed over the walls as I walked along, all the footie banners drawing my sight to the inside patio, where the bathroom was. I couldn't pee in the little room, nor think. It was too dark and I could barely move in there.

When I sat back I looked at the glass. It had a little beer in it. "7" continued right where we had left off like no time had passed. The bottle was empty.

—Hang on a minute –I called the barkeep over, pointing to the bottle, waving for another. I did the same with my glass. He didn't remember what wine I was drinking and before he got to me:

—Burgundy –then I turned to "7" and apologized for not listening and I asked him to continue where we had left off.

—C'mon! No... you gotta marry the person you love... I told the dude –"7" continued – You can't do that Coco, who is it? I asked him if he was still seeing his former girlfriend. No. Not her. The love of my life is someone else El Coco told me. You gotta tell that person that they're the love of your life. At least tell them... and like that the dude shoots... you, you're the love of my life. I was speechless.

I raised my hands just as the mustachioed barkeep stopped rubbing his belly. I asked for peanuts, fries and some cubed cheese. "7" drained his beer in one gulp. I refilled him instantly. He hadn't touched his mortadella sandwich; it overflowed with mayo and ketchup.

—There you go –I said.

—All good. It's that... I'm excited about what I'm telling you – said "7" as he wiped the froth from his mouth with the back of his hand. Like I said, nothing was making sense. Nothing Facu, nothing. The dude was in front of me, trashed, his eyes bloodshot, about to get married and telling me I was the love of his life... El Coco told me he imagined us old and together. That I'd never left him alone, that I'd always be by his side... and that he was gonna ask me to be godfather at his wedding.

There was a racket outside. At that moment it was getting harder to hear him. Tangos were blaring from the bar, one after another.

"Your house, your sidewalk and the canal / and an alfalfa and spice perfume / that fills again this heart of mine."

When the line dance ended, I heard him again as he had not been interrupted.

—Hang on... what happened? Did the dude get married or what? –I asked "7."

He stopped. Mute. We remembered we had a game in the morning. He banged his leg as he slid out of the chair. I had to help him walk. I looked at my watch. It was well past midnight. The cobblestone street was illuminated by the faint glow of the streetlights. He walked so hard into a tree pot he almost killed himself. I had to keep him up for a couple of blocks. He couldn't stay up.

He remembered the night he had to help Coco to his house cause he was so trashed he couldn't walk. He confessed, slurring his words, that it was the first time he had seen him naked. He had to take his shoes off, his pants, his shirt, even his briefs—because he had said they were too tight. He had flecks of drool and vomit on him. While "7" talked, he too drooled. I imagined myself taking off my friend's shoes, socks and pants. It would be the first time I would see him naked. But he was one of the boys from the squad... no way... I helped a couple more blocks. When we got to his door, he leaned into my shoulders and told me:

—There are things, that no matter how long ago they happened, you never forget, Facu. Are you gonna take care of me? At least until I find a boyfriend... —he said without really articulating his words.

—C'mon, go to bed and sleep –I said while pushing him inside and closing the door from the outside. I had just said bye with a kiss on the lips. They were wet with wine and spit. I still remember how he tasted. There are things, that no matter how long ago they happened, you never forget.

«8»
# TWO LOVERS

"8" is skinny and tall. He recently cut his hair. He has lived with his partner for fifteen years. He has no football skills, but he loves to play. He never misses training and he puts a lot of effort learning new tactics. He pays close attention to the indications that Coach gives him, and although it is hard for him to make the changes, he doesn't stop trying until he succeeds. According to Coach, he has perseverance and that is worth a lot.

—It's motivation… almost everything in football is wanting to do it, having guts…

—Yes, but if the guys don't come to training and instead go out to dance, then they can't get out of bed to come train. And if there is no technique, it ain't worth shit —added the "Physical Trainer."

"8" liked to speak like a woman before his accident in one of the matches of the last World Cup, where they broke his knee. He would scream: "Without me, without this Queen, you are nothing," he repeated this until we got tired of it. Now he has changed so much he seems like a different person. Never again did he refer to himself as a "she" since the day he met Jonathan. Jonathan is a 19-year-old kid. He distributes sodas in a Coca-Cola truck. He lives in La Boca, near the pitch. When he returns from work, he gathers with friends in the railroad tracks to smoke pot and drink beer. He wears a cap and gym pants. He hates gays, but with "8," it's a different story since the first day they met. "8" was looking for this guy named "Tubérculo" to buy joints and pills. When he came across Jonathan, he asked him if he knew the bloke. "8" was hypnotized as he saw Jonathan rub his abdominal muscles and remove his cap to respond:

—No. But if you want to, we can smoke this blunt I have here.

"8" in return, promised to download the list of cumbia *villera* tracks Jonathan gave him. And he kept his promise. The next day he appeared in the neighborhood on a bicycle, looking for him like crazy, with the CDs in a white envelope. Now our footie teammate changed from the disco Niceto, for El Kastillo, a cumbia club. He is teaching Jonathan how to play on Saturday afternoon. As far as I know, he doesn't know that "8" is gay; and according to him, it is the first time he hides it. He enjoys taking a ride on the bike's handlebars to smoke weed at Isla Maciel, or stay a couple of hours hanging, supported by his leg, with the sun behind. Or give him a hug when they say goodbye until the next day.

Particularity of "8:" he tries to hit on every critter that walks. One day, on errands near Chacarita, he got hot for a guy who was also in line at the bank. He stared at him hard until the kid got tired. The guy approached him as if he was about to punch him and yelled:

—Dude, what's wrong with you? Did I take something from you? What are you staring at, huh?

—No... no. It's that... that... that you remind me of my brother who died last year. You have no idea how much you resemble him. Seeing you is like seeing him, but he is dead, you see?

—Oh man... sorry... I didn't know. I'm so sorry... —he pressed his shoulder and continued to tell him:

—I also have a dead brother, but he doesn't resemble you at all...

Soon enough, "8" was already making suggestive looks to the waiter who worked in the corner pizzeria. When he told me the story, he also added:

—Why am I such a whore, Facu? I love cock so much, too much. I would suck all the dicks in the world. One by one, like ice cream. They are so beautiful... so different. Some are scented, others come uncircumcised that they even have cheese... and well, I won't even speak of sizes... and how they move them is the most important thing, you see?" I get so horny with strangers, to see what they have there... It's like a mystery, the most beautiful thing in the world... Sometimes I think that I became gay because I want to see every guy naked, to contemplate them. They are beautiful! ... their dicks, balls; and to suck them all up, all of them...

—And your partner? —I asked.

—Ah! That's another story… I love him. There is love with him.

—And your partner? —I asked again.

—I thought he was different. I had him on an altar. I was faithful to him the first years, until one day I came home early and found him in bed with two dudes. Not one, but two, Facu! And in our bed! I wanted to die. You don't know what that meant for me. I ended up in a mental hospital… From that day on the roles were reversed. He no longer goes on chat; he's always looking after me. He calls me a hundred times a day… Now, I thank him for what he did, because if it wouldn't have been for him, I wouldn't be the whore that I am today.

I didn't have more questions to ask. He had told me everything, or almost all of it.

## <<SUB 9>>
## NICE BOOTS

—Tie your laces, said the new guy to another as he passed him on a run. We were jogging, sweating profusely, along the Figueroa Alcorta avenue. We could see the traffic jam, moving like drained noodles in slow motion. The trees made a forest on the opposite sidewalk. I overheard someone say:

"Fucking is easy, you can get it right here, if you want. Finding love is the hard part."

I kept running and that statement kept looping in my thoughts. I kept running until I was a puddle of sweat.

"Fucking is easy, finding love is the hard part." "Fucking is easy, finding love is the hard part." It had been "3" who said it. But it couldn't've been him who came up with it. Maybe he heard it somewhere and was repeating it. I caught up with "4" to tell him. The guys who ran besides him heard it too. "Fucking is easy: finding love is the hard part," I told them like I was a radio transmission.

After warm-ups, I noticed that night was a little different than others. There was a ring around the moon that caught our eye. The guys from the country said the halo meant there'd be rain. The city boys, that we'd win on Sunday. Others said UFOs were coming. Two of the dudes said it was a magic ring that'd make our dicks grow. We laughed at that like we had smoked out.

The new guy took the "Sub 9" spot on the roster. He joined the team through "El Furia's" recommendation. He looked like the Green Lantern. He spat to his side and told "11" again:

—Dude, you haven't tied your boots yet! ... Hey, those are nice boots! Eh? Where'd you get 'em? How much?

We'd broken from the jog and were sprinting, I couldn't see the boots he was talking about. I'm sure they were a new type of turf cleats that looked a lot like the ones he had on.

"Turquesa" ran by, perky tits in a Boca jersey and a blue jean mini over his shorts; his hair dyed blonde, dry like hay, the dark roots showing; he sashayed brusquely. He pretended to be Wonder Woman sometimes. When "Sub 9" saw her pass, he yelled:

—There you go baby, you're beautiful! Keep running, you've almost caught the carrot! There's cock baby! It's waiting for you…

We looked at each other and paused for sec before we all started laughing uncontrollably.

The keeper leaned into me. As he neared, I smelled chocolate on his breath; he asked me:

—And this one? Where the fuck did he come from?

"Sub 9" kept saying:

—Damn this bitch is fine! Jesus, fire! Prime beef!

—Listen buddy, we're all friends here and we're here to have a good time. If you're horny, go whack one out –said "8." After a tense second he added, as a way of diffusing the moment –Or if you'd like, I can jerk you off.

"Sub 9" curled down his lips; he didn't say anything. His eyes shined in the darkness.

The game was intense. After recovery, Coach was blowing smoke up the new guy's ass:

—Guys, I want a welcoming round of applause for "Sub 9" for his excellent match. He gave his all and kept giving. I hope you follow his lead… you all saw what I'm always talking about, right? Be aware, make plays, exploit situations… play like wild stallions and not like show ponies. Here, it don't matter if you're gays, sluts, sword swallowers or whatever the fuck… Football is what brings us together, unites us, like balls! We have to win and play well. How did El Diego say it? It's more important to be a "9" than a "10." And why? Well, because a "9" will always have one step left to become a "10!" See? That's why he gave it his all! Good, welcome aboard sir!

We clapped with the same energy of a self-help group. We looked at each other. There was something we'd missed. Someone said:

—This fucking Coach, what bitch got a hold of him?

—Yeah, why's he lauding this asshole? Don't tell me he's in love with the new guy?

Some of the guys laughed.

It was 11:30 p.m. when we finished. Some of the guys wanted to catch a ride in the car with "Sub 9." Aside from the comments about "Turquesa" and the boots, he also said something nice about mine, he was a little timid, reserved. He was tall, good looking, short hair, with a milky complexion and light eyes.

—We're going to celebrate "Hisopo's" birthday at Angel's, wanna come? –asked "4" as he settled into the backseat.

—Alright.

—We'll meet up at one a.m. at the hot dog stand on Córdoba avenue and Junín. We'll see you there, if anything, take down my cell number. Just send me a text if anything.

—Is it cool if I bring my girlfriend?

—Yeah sure, if you want, that's cool. You can bring whoever you want. See ya –he got out of the car.

Before that, "Sub 9" gave everyone a goodbye kiss. He just extended his hand towards me, his pinkie out and said:

—See ya, cutie.

While the team danced upstairs (there was *cumbia* downstairs), "Sub 9" and his girl were arguing at a table on the landing between floors. When they finished fighting, he went to the bathroom and we didn't see him for a while. "4" told me the following morning, that he found him in the "dark" room.

—He was eating out a tranny's ass, up and down. They were flanked by a pair of muscular blonde guys who were making out. The room stank of shit and cheap cologne. One of the guys smelled rank, "4" went on to specify.

—The tranny's wig was bouncing around every time "Sub 9" pumped him. He was giving it to her in concentric circles, elliptically and the tranny was shrieking stutters like a cat in heat. He had her waist clenched and it looked like he was gonna come but he never finished. He'd take little rests on top of the tran's back and then he'd get back at it –said "4."

—There was a group of dudes looking on, jerking off, watching them fuck. And "Sub 9" kept at it, without finishing. He got faster and harder, like a washing machine picking up speed. He was in a trance. He took his cock out of her ass and that's when "4" saw it. White (a little rosy), fat and uncircumcised. One of the dudes made a grab for it. He batted away saying:

—"What the fuck dude? Don't touch… don't touch, I ah, I ah…" and he stuck it into her; she was still up, grabbing her ankles, her ass up in the air. He put it in deep and took it out completely, over and over again. He took it out slowly and jabbed it in quickly. You could hear her dry heave when he stuck it in. He finished with short, rhythmic movements, inside of her. He took the condom off and threw it aside and went directly to his table where his girl was talking to one of the guys from the squad.

—What the fuck, eh? I saw you… –he said.

—What? What the Hell is your problem? –said his girl as she turned to him.

—I saw you, don't fuck with me, ah? You were looking at that dickhead over there… and that one, that one over there.

—You've gone crazy…

—If I fucking catch you, eh? I'll kill you, eh? I'll kill you… –he said between clenched teeth as he squeezed her throat. We finished our beers and the few of us from the team who were left, went home. "Sub 9" left with his girl. "4" went home alone, as usual.

That Sunday we got together at "7's" apartment for the Argentina/Paraguay match. We drank a lot of beers. Argentina was losing. The guys were organizing an after party via text. Before the game ended, they left angry at the national team. "Sub 9" was the last to go. I left immediately. "7" told me that when there were five minutes of regulation time left, he changed the channel until he found something else he wanted to see.

—Ah, there, some pretty girls… that's what I need… this apartment stinks like balls dude.

—…

—Look at that chick; she looks like a doll, a slutty, dirty doll. Fuck, look at her bend over! She's got some moves. She can probably take it in deep. What a whore! –it was as if "Sub 9" was falling asleep the more he talked. He had a small tent in his gym shorts. He had slid one of his hands inside and took it out to smell it every so often. His tee was pulled back enough to see his six-pack and a thin line of his pubes creeping over the waistband.

"7's" heart started beating faster. He wanted to touch him but didn't dare. He was afraid "Sub 9" was gonna beat the shit out of him. Finally, he stopped thinking about it and gave in to his desire. He moved over to the couch and sat next to him. He closed his eyes and slowly caressed his cock over the shorts. "Sub 9" grabbed his hand and pulled it under his shorts. He kept his eyes closed, making soft noises that blended in with his breathing. He was either asleep or drunk. He started rubbing it up and down. He spat on his hand and rubbed his dickhead. He stretched his legs. He opened them and slid between. It looked like he was falling unto the floor. He covered his face with a Boca cap. Once "7" sucked the cum out of him, which didn't take long to flow, "Sub 9" fell asleep. "7" went to the bathroom. He didn't know whether to rub his tongue or wash it. When he saw him asleep on the couch, like a sack of potatoes, Maradona tattooed on his ankle, he suddenly wanted him to leave. But he didn't wake him.

At six in the morning, "Sub 9" startled him in the kitchen as he made coffee. He told him he was leaving, that he had fallen asleep.

—See ya buddy –as he gave him his hand. When the hands met, there was a loud noise outside.

—C'mon, I gotta let you out.

As they went down in the elevator, "Sub 9" looked at the floor. He said:

—Dude, wanna change boots? I'll bring them back to practice on Tuesday. I promise.

"7" pressed "ground floor" again.

They sat on a step in the building's lobby and changed shoes. They were both Nike turf boots. "Sub 9's" were white leather, considerably worn with light blue lines on the sides. "7's" looked a little bigger, more detailed with more color but they weren't leather.

"Sub 9" exited the building. Crossed the empty street and walked to the other end of the avenue. "7" closed the door to the building. As he walked into his apartment, he remembered something "Sub 9" had asked one of the guys during the Argentina game:

—Dude, let me see your tires.

"7" went straight to his room. There was stuff everywhere. He counted how many pairs of shoes he had. There weren't any missing. He tried to sleep, couldn't. He looked out of the balcony and saw "Sub 9" at the 36 stop on his phone. "Surely he was talking with his girl," said "7" later that day.

The following Tuesday, when we were in the La Quemita lockers, "Sub 9" kept cracking jokes at "5," one of the straight guys on the team. He had a body built in a gym, well-defined, hairless, baby-faced with a donkey's cock.

—Come here big boy... wash my cock... when you learn how to play, you'll have my spot. Meanwhile, you gotta suck my toes... did you see that pass I gave you? Well, I hope you never forget it dude. Don't be an ingrate... c'mon wash my balls... c'mon homie, with that mandingo, you must drive the bitches crazy, right? You get it, right? Guys like you and me, we're both... we like chicks... one of these days we oughtta go out and hook up with a real slut... ha ha – he laughed and turned away. He had his back to us under the showerhead. I guess he didn't want us to see that he had gotten hard. Truth be told; he wasn't as good a player as he'd been sold to us. We canceled the next two trainings and we didn't tell him. We never saw "Sub 9" again save for a lone photo you can still see on the web.

# <<9>>
# SUBSTITUTIONS

He was still logged on, even though his roommates told him it was late. The rest of the team was already asleep. The lights were off.

It was two in the morning and he was still chatting with his boyfriend, who was 64, and his mom, (he spoke with her every day). The loud sighs of annoyance from "8," "11," "17," plus mine, did not stop. Every-now-and-then they piggy-backed an insult, and sounds of restlessness from one of the beds. "11" covered his head with a pillow to block the glare from the screen that washed over the whole room.

Before traveling to the championship in Córdoba, "9" had a rash that started when he had shaved his head. He broke it off with his long-term boyfriend with whom he had lived with for a few years and quit his job. He'd been a machinist at a factory in Escobar for five years and was now 32 years old. After his "breaks," he started eating everything he could lay his eyes on. He put on 24 pounds in three months. We started calling him "Homer Simpson's Clone." He went from a chive to an artichoke. His character changed too. He had turned grumpy, full of irony and hostility. He'd always been a little dumb and careless.

One afternoon, returning from Sarmiento Park, my daughter asked if "9" was gay.

—It's that he doesn't look it, daddy.

—And why not?

—Cause… did you see how he threw the laptop onto the backseat? He doesn't take care of things… he's not neat like the others… he brakes suddenly… he's got that gruff voice… he picks his nose and he grabs his wee-wee when he talks.

"And he's passive my dear…" I thought. But didn't say because she wouldn't get the joke. "He's never gotten into anyone, he can't get it up," I kept thinking.

That night in Córdoba we held a meeting in the bathroom. "9" was still chatting away, his fingers a blur on the keyboard. "11" sat on the border of the tub. He was the first to speak up:

—What the fuck are we gonna do about this asshole? We have a game tomorrow. We have to be up by six thirty for breakfast and…

—Yes, and then the therapist takes us for warm-ups at the park, and… —said "17" with obvious concern.

—We're gonna be dead for the match and we want to win… this is fucked —protested "8."

—I'm going to break my foot kicking his ass, now. And I'm gonna leave him all fucked up on the floor. If he wants to keep chatting, he's gotta go out to the hallway —I said finally, exasperated.

When we got back to the room, we noticed the door ajar, like we had left it. The light from his screen no longer a beacon in the dead of dark. His laptop was off. So was his light. There was no sound. "8," "11" and "17" went in quietly so as to not wake "9." I followed. "11" walked into something that fell unto the floor with a loud thud.

—I think it's someone's deodorant, I'm sure. Go ahead, leave it, it doesn't matter —whispered "8" —let's go to sleep, it's late.

We had broken a bottle of Armani cologne that "9" had bought at the mall the day before while the rest of looked at boots, shin guards and team jerseys. The smell was strong.

—Fuck him, he's always been a jerk —I thought.

The four of us went to sleep, each one on his bed, but we didn't sleep well. The first light that peeked through the blinds showed "9's" bed, empty. The sun looked like a tangerine.

While we ate breakfast, we found out that "9" had broken up with the team too.

The game without him went well. Without his grumpiness and bad attitude, we could enjoy the game from the bench. From that night on we were able to sleep. We had gotten rid of a considerable weight.

*The wide open blue sky followed us until it turned black and thick. Like Mariano Blatt would say: it was our friend.*

## <<SUB 10>>
## WHEN MOLECULAR FOOD IS TRANSFORMED INTO HOTDOGS

**1**

—I like dicks so much —said the sub, putting on his jersey with the number "10" on his back, before entering the pitch. –Why do I like it so much? He asked again while stretching, ready to play.

"Sub 10" is from Neuquén. He came to live in Buenos Aires to study cooking. He is about to get his degree as a chef. He likes gourmet cooking, molecular cuisine and new recipes; but what he enjoys the most is preparing hotdogs with mustard. Sometimes, when we are back from a night of clubbing we stay over at his place if we happen to have practice the next day.

The first day he came to see us, he had met our team online, he looked shy, almost afraid. "The Fury" asked bluntly:

—What about you, dude, what's up? —but he just stared at him.

—What do you mean what's up? He managed to say with a broken tone, like a loose thread.

—Active or passive?

—Active, "Sub 10" said trying to put on his manliest voice, although it was not necessary.

—Active with the ass, replied "10," while he was turning and shaking his butt. We could not believe it. We looked at each other trying to cool down the situation, but not knowing how to handle it. We did not want "Sub 10" to leave without playing or not come back. But we could not talk because we couldn't stop laughing. "Sub 10" had a cold expression in his face, swallowing his saliva trying to hide the string of ants running through his body.

Almost a year later, "Sub 10" began spitting things out, without thinking, whatever came to his mind, like he was Johnny Bravo. One night, in the house of "7" when "Starting 10" asked "Sub 10" how he had started sexually, he told us:

—In the country side, the town where I was born. When my mom sent me out to run some errands, there was a kid, a little bigger than me, I would've been... I don't know, twelve or thirteen years old. The boy looked at me and said things. He was standing at a corner. One day, when I ran into him, I got so nervous I dropped the potatoes, the yams, everything I had in my bag. The dude helped me put them back in and as we walked to my house I started to feel lots of things. I realized that I was afraid of the guy. But he was nice. However, he would look straight at me and I tried to avoid him. He had incredible blue eyes, and their intensity bothered me. It made me nervous. The kid just wanted to be friends with me. He had a log between his legs. He would adjust it all the time and that also made me nervous. Then, when I went home with the groceries and we passed by the grasslands, I threw myself on top of him. Just like that, without thinking. The kid was creeped out. I remember that at some point he grabbed me by the chin and looking straight into my eyes asked, "what are you doing, dude?" I was shaking. I thought he was going to fuck me up. I did not say anything. I felt my mouth dry. After a while, he said to me, "you're crazy, brother, but well ... what do you want to do?" I didn't know what to say. So, I didn't say anything. He pointed at his dick with his finger and smiled at me, "well, jerk me off," and took out his dick, which was huge even though it was flaccid. Then he said, "I'll suck you off, but you gotta suck me first." I did not want to... but he pushed my head down to it.

The water was boiling and the hotdogs were exploding. The bell rang. There were hotdogs all over. More people came to the house. The TV was on with the Real Madrid game and the speakers played an old song by The Cure.

I missed a piece of the conversation or the monologue:

—What I wanted most was for the dude to hug me and stay with me in the grasslands or make a little house on top of a tree. I grabbed him by the waist and leaned on his belly. The kid pushed me and I ran out. Later on, when I'd run into him, I would cross the street or I would not say hello. What an idiot, right? A few months later I saw him at a dance club. He was making out with Lorena, a girl from my class.

"Sub 10" was still talking, but nobody was listening. The boys hugged the newcomers. Someone stumbled onto the coat rack and the jackets spilled across the floor.


**2**


This weekend is "10's" birthday; and "Sub 10" promised to prepare the best food he has ever tasted.

—What are we going to eat?

—It's a surprise —said "Sub 10."

—Go on, tell me... doggie-dogs?

—If I suck a new dick today, I'll tell you. Otherwise, not.

—Look at you! The first day you joined the team we thought you weren't even gay... you're quite the little slut now!

—Ha ha ha. Look, I'll tell you what I'd like to make for your birthday: dick broth. Put all the cocks you can fit in a pot and let it simmer. Add a little cheese and eggs ... and some carrots.

—Know something? I kick your ass on the field, that's why I'm the starter and you are the sub; but you might be better in bed after all. Bah! I guess... Do you like big cocks?

—I like them all, doc.

—What about this one?

—Hmm... I think I'll make you a nice cock for Saturday.

From that day on we had one less problem. The rivalry between "Sub 10" and "Starting 10" was gone. They started dating and didn't care who played as a starter or as substitute. They were acquiring the same gestures and features. Sometimes we got confused and changed the names. Now the two seem to be the same person.

## <<10>>
## THE DOC'S IDEA

Sitting on the tiled roof of "7's" house, we smoked a joint. We listened to the silence. We didn't care about the time. We saw the lights of the city turn on like balloons that were inflated and we were surprised. We jumped off the terrace. We took beers that had been cooling in some buckets. We chased them with the Fernet & Coke prepared by "Parasite," "8's" boyfriend. Later we uncorked a couple of expensive wines (Rutini, Catena Zapata, Alta Vista) gifted to the Doc by his beloved patients. We brought more beers from the tub below, where they floated among ice packs.

With his feet soaking in the hot tub and a glass of champagne in his hand, "10" who is a physician, began to speak. I thought about how important his world was: he worked at the General Hospital, in a private clinic in San Isidro, and as a professor at a private university, where he held a tenured chair.

He told us that five years ago, he produced a show where he danced with a tutu, without underpants and with wooden pasties in the shape of cones. The show consisted in walking faster and faster to almost running, and at the least expected moment, he would jump on top of his partner, who weighed more than a hundred kilos. He lifted him with his arms up, making him turn like the blades of a fan and then threw him on top of the audience, who looked on with surprise. The second part of the show was a kind of Dirty Dancing, but with mixed roles. "10," dressed as a man, tried to climb Fat Lucas, who was dressed as a woman, in the air. The failed attempts multiplied in slapstick gags where they'd end up falling to the floor like dolls without batteries.

They did that show for years, at private parties and queer discos. They're like different people today.

"10," in addition to his responsibilities on the field and being "Sub 10's" boyfriend, is heading the team's extra-curricular activities. He organizes the team to visit children with terminal illnesses such as HIV, cancer and others at the hospital. We bring them toys we spend an afternoon playing footie with them at the hospital's pitch. Sometimes, we give them signed t-shirts by the team. The last weekend we visited, a little boy with his shaved head and on his last chemo session, asked us if we were a queer team. We had put up the rainbow flag behind the goal. He confronted us before the presentation we were about to give, where we told them who we are, what we do and why we worked with integration and diversity. When "The Doc" kicked back the question as if it were a ball, the boy asked us why we had put the flag and we had baseball caps with so many colors. While we drank chocolate milk with vanilla, the boy told us that his sister was also gay, and that he would like us to make friends with her because she was lonely.

—This seven-year-old kid spoke better than us —said the keeper with a smile.

—Being close to death and being aware that you are going to die makes you wake up, think clearly and understand things better... those things happen to you.

—I have to die then —said "8."

—Shut up, dumbass —quipped "Sub 10."

—You accept things as they are, without prejudice —continued Doc. Besides, that's the way kids are, spontaneous, sincere.

Every time he spoke everyone listened. Maybe that's why he finished his statements with some kind of joke or did some funny gesture or something at the end.

"The Doc" was drunk the night of the get-together. With his body fully immersed in the Jacuzzi, he told us about putting on that show from the 90's he did with his friend, Fat Lucas, at the hospital that he worked at.

—But... What about the Chief of Staff? What will he say? —asked his scared boyfriend.

—And your coworkers? Can you imagine them? You have to think about the day after... Are you sure what you're saying, man?

—You are joking, right! You're drunk —said the goalie— you look like Pinky, from the cartoons my little brother was watching...

—To hell with everything and everyone. I'm free and I'm happy, my sweets —said "The Doc" as if he were speaking from a stage with hundreds of people watching him, eager to know the end.

He stretched out his hand. He took the cell phone that was next to a pack of cigarettes, and called Lucas. He spoke in English and he was laughing. When he hung up, he told us:

—All taken care. Next Saturday we rehearse and we'll do it.

To celebrate we threw ourselves onto him, in the water. We crushed him. I couldn't breathe. Nor did we let him take off his head out to take a breath. He swallowed water. He turned red and started coughing. He gagged.

—Should we call an ambulance? —said "7" bringing more champagne while singing from a Charly García song "Please ... don't die in my house..."

"Doc" came out of the water blowing his nose and stated:

—Who wants to help me? I'm gonna start rehearsals right now.

"4" who was a solid bloke, helped him. We smoked some more and laughed.

When we went down the elevator I asked him what was his need to do the show at his work?

—I don't give a shit, Facu. I got tired of hiding all the time. Doc here, Doc there. Hiding my boyfriend to my mom... And what about me? The person who I am? I don't count?

—If you want to tell your co-workers that you are gay, you should do it. Okay? But the show seems to have nothing to do with it, but that's just me...

—Yeah. That's what I want. Break with the serious image of inspector that I have, of asexual, boring bachelor who lives with his mother. They confuse me with a fern, Facu...

—If you want, we can do the show at the Children's Hospital the next time we go and we can count how many smiles the kids make and we can pick them up with a tiny spoon and stuff them into the Coach's mouth —I said, knowing he was high as fuck. On the sidewalk there was a little girl making circles with a sparkle in the air. The silver sparks left a tail of smoke.

—Yes. That's what I want to do! —I had forgotten what we had been talking about. —And with all due respect to my co-workers, since I'm tired of them trying to hook me up with chicks, I'm gonna send them a Facebook message telling them that I'm fucking gay. Whether they like it or not ... Imagine what I'm gonna stir, Facu.

—¿...?

—A mass suicide, of disappointed women. They can suck my dick. I will upload the team photos to Facebook and I will tell everyone where I play. Also, the one where I'm kissing with "Sub 10." I'm sick of it. It's over. I want to take a load off of my shoulders. Now, let's swim, smoke and suck dick, we don't know when the world ends. And if not, look at what happened in Fukushima.

<<11>>
## THE SON OF THE MILITARY MAN

He's a family man. Has two sons and a girl. Calls the older one "Flogger." He spends his time uploading photos to the Internet. The players say that "11" has a gay son. We laugh and he laughs too. He never gets mad. His father is an active military man. On Sundays, after the game, "11" and his children have lunch at Carmen's house, his mother. With increasing frequency, he invites some of us over for a meal. At the table, the father seems more masochistic than sadistic, we say, trying to make sure "11" doesn't hear what he's actually thinking. When we make a joke he doesn't understand, he looks down, embarrassed. Sometimes he stays out of the conversation.

A few months ago, "11" made the decision to separate from his wife. After lots of talking and thinking about it, they came to an agreement. A while before, with the excuse to give his ex something to do or make some money, he opened a grocery store for her in the same block as his house. Now we follow the Physical Trainer's advice: eat a fruit after training, to replenish energy and to not wear out the muscles. During the summer, "11" appeared with bags full of tangerines and bananas. On several occasions we threw him to the floor, dogpiling hugs on him, scattering the fruits about the park.

His wife always knew that her husband was bisexual, but she did not care. All she asked was that he didn't leave her. In her begging she would put the children in the middle. She stated that they were not going to understand him, that Ricardo was going to die of a heart attack if he found out the reason for the separation; and other things like that.

"11's" first love was a boy of 21, when he was the same age. They were close friends until they started having sex in hiding. Their girlfriends also became friends; they had introduced them. The four hung out on Saturday nights. They shared lunches, movies and went to football matches at *La Bombonera*. But this was short-lived, since Julián,

"11's" friend, killed himself driving on the highway. He lost control and crashed into a rail guard causing the accident. He died instantly. It was really hard for "11" to deal with that loss. He was depressed for a long time and still now, he says, has a hard time getting over it. After Julián's death, "11" told us between *mate* and *dulce de leche* pastries, that he'd been faithful to his wife for many years while repressing his gay desires. They started sleeping in separate beds. "11" couldn't stand the smell of the body of the mother of his children, or her proximity. It was a rejection that became more pronounced with the passage of time. But at times, he liked his wife's company, she had things in common with his mother. He had become used to it, as one gets used to taking the bus. She was someone who "was there," regardless of what he said or did. She would take anything, as long as he did not leave her. She even told him that if he wanted to have a lover over, she would put the kids to sleep and leave him the master bedroom. At night she cooked his food. She looked after the children. She took them to the school and picked them up after. She did the groceries. She cleaned the house. She made the bed just as "11" liked, because he had his pet-peeves. She even called him on his cell phone when she saw him sad or when he was late. He'd met her at Julián's house. He had already made out with her once. "11" distributed chickens in a truck in the outskirts of Buenos Aires and in the city.

After a while, he began chatting online with blond guys, short and stocky like chickens. Sometime after, he realized that they shared the same characteristics as his dead friend. Soon he fell in love with one of them. This time, the short and blond guy in the photo turned out to be tall, dark and big. He didn't care. Agustín was living a similar life: he had a girlfriend and a best friend with whom he had had sex with secretly and later had abandoned him. After that, he couldn't bear to enter the house anymore and greet Marta. She had gotten ugly.

—Fat, always wearing the same sweatpants, her hair a mess and dirty, her pussy stank —he told me.

He hated to see her in flip flops, with her toenails unpainted. Her way of walking bothered him, how she dragged her feet, how she moved her rough hands from washing the dishes and selling vegetables. He hated her hoarse voice, on the verge of crying, the look of constant concern. However, he never said anything offensive to her; keeping the growing rejection and disgust to himself. Deep down, he still loved her. He felt sorry for her, but he was used to her company. At that time, he didn't know if he was even willing to leave her. Also, he was incapable of hurting her.

When they separated, he went back to his parents' house. He enjoys where he lives now. He loves drinking *mates* with his mom in the morning, and respecting his father's silence during dinner. He's happy sleeping again in his childhood bedroom, visiting his children in the afternoons, taking them to school. When "11" drives his truck, full of chicken boxes, he gets upset if someone honks. When he traveled with the team to play the Gay World Cup in the United States, he let other players borrow his tablet, he would pay for recharges on Skype Voice so they could contact their partners. When we returned to Buenos Aires, he made each one of us a CD with all the photos from the trip.

Once, after practice, I was cold and was sweating. I asked his permission to change inside the truck. That time the truck had a different perfume than the usual chicken smell. It was a fresh smell. "11" showed me the "Paraguay Jasmine" flowers that were in the windshield.

The next training, he showed up with the plant that I'd liked. His mom had grown it from a cutting. He carried it in a paint can wrapped in a bag with soil and humus. Carmen had seen me several times at her house, but always confused me with other guys on the team. She was a religious fanatic who put Jesus stamps everywhere. She had an altar with the Virgin who, according to her, she'd seen cry. "Maybe she was on her period," I said one day to "11" and he pissed himself laughing. That afternoon, with the plant in hand, I gave my friend a hug that was hard to end.

When we received the polls from our Facebook survey, asking about for best gay of the year, under "Nobility and Qualities of a Good Person," 25 of us had voted for him. I nicknamed him "Benito Bodoque," like the blue, good-looking cat, from the Top Cat cartoon. I used to watch that show on telly, any morning I missed school. But it was from the 70's and almost nobody knew the reference, so we kept calling him "11."

This Saturday he will tell his father that he is part of an "unconventional" squad, where he works with diversity and that his condition is to be 100% passive. That he only fucks 21-year-old boys, he jokes. He says he is going to say that he likes to get it from behind, legs on shoulders or doggy-style, that he likes to get his head stroked like a dog when he gets fucked. Then he asks: "How will my old man take it?"

*Almost every end-of-year, after scrimmages, we'd go eat at the pizzeria at the Barrancas de Belgrano train station. The waiters knew all of us. The first day, after they recognized us, we ended up signing autographs and some of us sucked dicks in the bathroom.*

## <<12>>
## BLOOD IN THE EYE


On the pitch he has the uncanny ability to kick the ball to the opposite side the goalie throws himself to. Sometimes, he comes drunk, but on the pitch he transforms and is remarkable, better than most of us. He is charming and seductive. Once he's fucked someone, he doesn't want to fuck them anymore, regardless of how much he likes the guy. He only picks strangers to sleep with and lots of them have asked him to elope. This summer a Brazilian guy invited him to come and live in Rio de Janeiro with only one condition: that he leave behind everything he knows: his friends, the team and football. He never finished high school, and he doesn't work, he doesn't have a boyfriend or family (at least that we know of). He's skinny, brunette, dark-skinned and has an afro. We joke with him that he looks like Valderrama and he says he's more like Ronaldo. He's always laughing and showing that busted tooth. He's happy and fun. Sometimes, he doesn't listen. In those cases, we repeat what we say and shake him a little to let him know we are serious, but he still ignores us. He stays in his world, to himself, lost in it.

He travels quite a bit. Every now and then, we hear about some of the remote places he's been to, although we don't really know what happens there. He lives in the Buenos Aires province. Sometimes, he says in San Martin, other times in Haedo or Castelar. A kid that joined our team said he was from Ramos Mejia; and, since "12" seems to know all of the Western hoods, he asked and re-asked details:

—Do you know the Coto supermarket by the station? How many blocks are you from there?

Now it seems that he also lives in Hurlingham. The strange thing is that it never occurred to us to question him and say to him:

—Dude, do you live in all the West-side neighborhoods?

He loves to eat celery with golf sauce everywhere he goes, including out in the streets. He's got a tight, hard ass like a duck (sometimes we call him Daffy Duck), super defined abdominal muscles and when he gets nervous one of his eyes goes a little lazy. He has tattooed several little stars on his leg and the Huracán crest above his cock. With this tattoo, he is trying to cover a scar he got as a kid. We've asked him several times about it and every time he downplays the importance of it:

—I fell off my bike and stabbed myself with the handlebars.

The skin there looks like a wrinkled bed sheet, and in the summer it gets darker than usual. He worked at a greengrocer in Barrio Norte, and in a fire extinguisher factory and is currently unemployed. While painting the fire extinguishers at the factory he was hospitalized. He said he inadvertently poisoned himself with the paint. A friend of ours asked us to go and visit him because he was in seriously ill. He passed through intensive care. He had Hepatitis B and venereal diseases: syphilis and some other ones I forgot. Luckily, he wasn't HIV positive.

One evening when we were coming back from Villa de Mayo, we shared the same car. "12" took out a wallet full of foreign currency: guaraníes or Uruguayan money. He asked me where I thought he could change them, and how much they'd give him. That night he had been partying it with a consul and his friends at an embassy. I never knew if he'd earned or stolen the money. And even though I leaned towards the second hypothesis, I was never able to confirm my suspicions. He took out a Tommy cologne, an Armani shirt and a brand-new cell from his backpack. Neither I or the other guys in the car asked.

One day, he told me he had been with a Swedish guy in the Axel Hotel. After drinking champagne by the pool, they went to his room and the Swede asked him to spit on him. When he obliged, the Swede began to punch him in the face while his dick got rock hard. I don't know if that was the strangest experience he's had, but it's the one he told us while we changed in the Defensores de Belgrano locker room because he couldn't hide the bloodied black eye. We were about to take the pitch against "The Famous" and he couldn't see shit.

## <<13>>
## HE'S COMING ON A MOTORBIKE

He came to our scrimmages on a motorcycle. He had a Simpson's sticker on the gas tank. He was skillful with the ball, but a person of few words. We gave him the nickname, "Mr. Motorcycle." During our barbecues he would carry the bags of bread from the pickup to the table. He would clean the grill, wash the vegetables, and salt the meat while the couple from Entre Rios lit the fire.

The night that we got together to eat at "7's" house, "13" showed up with a tower of ready-to-eat pizza dough that his wife kneaded for us and a Tupperware for the tomato sauce; in another were the diced tomatoes and green olives. He'd gone to live with her in a building in Flores, about six years ago, around the same time that he joined the team. No one knows too much about his life except this: he's married and he roots for Independiente. He works at a gay disco. He started working in the coat room. Then, he went on to helm one of the bars in the club. Later, they promoted him to floor manager. The few times we saw him in action, we realized he was not crazy about his promotion. When he lived in the U.S., with his wife, he also played on a queer team. The team respects him and even admires him. After scrimmaging, the first person who asks, he gives them a ride home. When he's MVP of a match, we ask him for footballing advice. He responds with one or two words, but he never reveals the secret.

One Sunday afternoon, while he was getting on his motorcycle and asking me to put my backpack on my chest instead of my back, we talked with a little more ease.

—There are no formulas for this Facu, you just have to have fun on the pitch. Open your eyes and play. Nothing more. There are no secrets —the wind beat us on the face. My eyes started to water. When the light changed to green, he peeled out. It proved impossible to talk past Rivadavia and José María Moreno, where he dropped me off so I could buy the newest Franz Ferdinand CD, the one I hadn't been able to download from the Internet.

One afternoon, the kid that had most recently joined the team, asked him point blank:

—If you're straight, why do you play on a gay team?

—Because I like to play, champ, and on the pitch we are all the same... What's the importance of what you do in bed? That doesn't change a thing... We are here to play and have fun, are we not?

The kid with glasses, who'd just come out of the closet and was Bowie's spitting image, insisted. "13" already looking like "Furia" said:

—What? Now you are going to hate on me because I am hetero? —and he began to juggle the ball while asking this question. He passed it to the guys who were changing into their kits. Looking at one side of the goal he screamed:

—C'mon guys, run, play!

"Gender doesn't unite us; what unites us are the obstacles that we overcome in our lives," Coach used to say, who was also hetero. When he used to say that we used to run to him and hug him until we all fell down.

"7" would tease "13," telling him that he was his husband. He would grab him by the arm and fill it up with kisses. He wouldn't say anything but would put on a face of repugnance. But he liked to feel loved. Whenever he saw a girl, his eyes would inevitably wander over her tits and ass.

—It's in his nature, like monkeys or horses —"7" would bellow in a resignation, and we would all laugh.

—Playing is already quite a goal —"13" would say to anyone who got onto the game day roster. Being together is already a win —he'd tell me in a hush.

—Don't pass it to that guy, he's straight! —yelled Bowie, trying to be funny.

—Don't discriminate... don't discriminate... don't discriminate... —our unified chant was heard, in crescendo, as if it was coming from the bowels of the ocean.

—There are lots of stories and conjectures that were created in relation to the motive of why "13" played with us. One time, I heard someone say that he played with us because his school friends had tortured an effeminate classmate by locking him in the bathroom. They kicked the shit out of him and spat on him. Supposedly, to reaffirm his masculinity and not be less than anyone else, "13" played into this sadism. They say he was the one that fucked him up while the rest held the kid down. Bowie (who abandoned the team the same week that he appeared) supposed our friend has a gay brother, that his parents didn't accept him and they ended up throwing him out of the house, with his complicity. That he's never seen him again, and that's why he played with us.

None of these theories have been proven. I think that "13" doesn't know why he plays with us, but he plays well. After a game, when a journalist fingered at him:

—You're the hetero on the team —having guessed correctly and waiting for the rest of us to praise his "gaydar;" "13's" face transformed. He looked at the up-until-then-cool journalist intently, without lowering his gaze. Like saying:

—And you, aren't you writing an article against discrimination?

When the lights turned off and the cameras left, "7" gave him a hug. "13's" mom, who'd been sitting in the bleachers, celebrating every clearance that stamped out the offence's advance; missed his best play: "13's" silence in front of the journalist's question.

That part was edited and never seen on TV.

*Why is it that one ends up loving what they hated most?*
*We promoted divisions in the tourney and now play in the Nacional A. We miss the smell of piss in the locker-room and the rusted and dilapidated lockers, the showers with their sad dribble hitting us on our shoulders. Showering without soap and barefoot… even feeling sad after a loss, getting together to talk shit under the blackberry tree, the same old things we always did.*

## <<14>>
## THE WISH IS ANOTHER'S WISH

1

Between jogs and the stretch session, "14" told me:

—I don't know if I should call him back or not.

—Why?

—Were you listening?

—Look, as far as I'm concerned, you're gonna like what you're gonna like, right? ... I like dudes with mean faces, so what? The thuggier the better...

—Sure dude, but this one's too much...

—I don't know, he doesn't seem so bad to me, to tell the truth —I said without really remembering the last dude he'd hooked up with.

—You know what's the last thing he told me?

—...

—To leave my socks on for a whole week, so they'd get get stinky so he could suck on them later and jack off into them.

—Ha ha ha.

—No way, this motherfucker's crazy...

—...

—He says that with another guy he met through chat, they would smell shit together. The guy would get it together and rub it on his nose...

—You're fucking with me...

—No, no, I'm serious. They kicked him out of the gym he was going to cuz they caught him... He says he'd wait until the guys there would hit the showers and he'd steal their underwear. He'd hide them in his bag and would jerk off at home while smelling them. He told me in a chat that the more you smelled, the better your sense of smell became. That's how he'd gotten such a large range of senses. He could recall the smell of balls, dicks and even the ass of whatever underwear he'd sniff. Even a whole week after taking them.

—And… what are you gonna do? —I asked.

—I don't know; I'm dying to meet him… the photos he sent me are so good…


2


"14," the keeper and I, who'd gotten to practice late, had to join a horizontal row, where the guys were shoulder-to-shoulder. Then we numbered ourselves:

—One, two, three. ONE, two, three. One, two (with a girl's voice), three (loudly).

—Without jokes please… —said the trainer while Coach lined up a row of balls for the next exercise. The orange cones were already lined up in place.

When we finished, we split up into three groups of eight to do the circuits. Coach gave us two minutes to rest, timed on his stopwatch. "10" and the keeper, who'd heard some of our conversation, joined us.

—I… I don't know… I don't think traditional sex would happen with this guy…

—Yeah… no. How old is he?

—He's a jit, I think 18, or 19. Dark, but he's not a black guy. Short hair. Good body. Baby-faced. I'm fascinated by him… but I also got someone else I'm looking at.

—…

—His name is Lucas. He says he went to Europe last year with his family; he still lives at home. He told me that one night, in a sauna in either Barcelona or Madrid, I don't remember, well, whatever, whatever city he was in… he found… —Coach blew the whistle.

We stretched out with a leg on the ground and the other atop a small mountain of rocks, the ones that surround the tree a few meters from the Güimes Monument. The keeper came running and got between

"14" and "5." He looked at "5" and winked. I switched spots so I could hear "14," who kept talking:

    —Where was I? I told you about the poop?

    —Yeah, you were telling us the dude went to Barcelona.

    —Ah, yes! He said he was coming out of a sauna, and while he walked down the hallway, half-naked, he came across his dad, also half-naked with only a towel covering him…

    —Nah? C'mon, you're fucking with us?

    —No man, for real I'm telling you…

    —Those chat stories are bullshit…

    —For real, bah! Whatever… he told me his old man turned suddenly and made for the exit. Lucas stayed there. Hooked up with a dude. After he showered and changed, as he was leaving… you won't guess who he bumped into on the way out?

    —… No…!

    —Yup…

    —So what happened?

    —Nothing. He was there with the mom and the other kids. They left together for dinner at some super fancy place… Ha ha ha. Well, what do I do about the underwear sniffer with the super nose?

    —You like this guy that much?

    —I… I don't know… I like Lucas, but the other guy excites me. I think I'd be able to do things I'd never have a chance to do or try…

    —What's his name?

    —Junior.

    —Junior?

    —Yeah, he's Brazilian.

    —Yeah, you told me already… why'd he come here?

    —To study how to be a chef… I don't know if I should meet up… I'm a little nervous… but deep down I want to… I'm dying to have him… smell me all over… he's super fucking dirty —"14" stopped. He looked at me and kept talking —you get me? He says he has more than thirty pairs of underwear at home. He never washes them. He still jerks off to the smell of cock and balls of strangers…

    —Yeah, you said that, but… how's his cock? —asked the keeper.

—What? You wanna fuck him?

—No, dumbass… You see how this is? Maybe I've crossed paths with him… and…

—If you'd met him already, you'd remember. He's incredible. Well, to tell the truth… we've already seen each other, once.

We had to pick up the balls and bag them. Also the cones. We drank some water, ate the cereal bars we had, and then while seated in a circle, Coach read the roster sheet for Sunday's match. We had to be quiet. The keeper told me in passing:

—That's incredible what I just heard! It's going round and round in my mind.

—Yo! Dude, do I got you on Facebook? —the keeper asked "14."

—Yeah, for sure.

—Your lovers on there too?

—The majority of them I guess… why?

—No, nothing, just to check that dude out… I'm curious about guys like that. That type of personality. Specially that, Lucas was it? How crazy is that? You go to a meat market and find your dad. Imagine if it had been a dark room!

We had the last part of the training ahead. We had ten minutes to do the cool down. All 24 of the guys were jogging in groups, but not in order. Trying to listen in on the guys, I ran up a bit. I reached them in time to hear the keeper tell "14:"

—Sex is easy. Finding love is the hard part —I heard that before, from one of the guys, during another training session. It was déjà vu. Whenever "El Furia" was in good spirits, he'd say: "I said it or I thought it." I didn't know if I had lived it or if I had dreamt it.


3


"14" and the keeper missed Tuesday's training session. A few days later, we found out through a series of e-mails, that they had had a major fight. They told me that the keeper, through chat, got in touch with Junior. He asked him out. The next day, when "14" finally made up his mind to call him, even after the keeper advised him not to, Junior told him he had met someone and that it was too late... When he described the new man in his life, he realized who'd gotten the upper hand here.

<<15>>
## FATHER AND SON TANGO

"15's" dad is a huge tango fan. He even works as a dance instructor at a *milonga*. He's an avid collector of Carlos Gardel vinyl. He roots for River and goes to every Sunday match with the religious zeal of mass. He's limited when it comes to expressing himself, but deep down inside, he's a little fragile and sensitive. His ex-wife, "15's" mom, from what I could hear during one of our playdates at his home, says she's a medium; even talks to the dead and sees the auras of the souls that pass through her. She's medicated. They commit her sometimes, when one of the souls gets stuck inside of her.

"15's" a huge fan of *El Flaco* Spinetta. He's got a tattoo of Almendra's first album on his arm. He likes to write, read, go to the theater, the movies, recitals and generally enjoys anything in the arts. He's up-to-date on sporting news and soccer.

A few years ago, he wrote a script for a soap that was produced in Paraguay and some articles for a gay magazine. Now he works for an NGO and gives lectures at schools in favor of diversity and against discrimination.

He's got a lot of friends but is a little reserved when it comes to forming deeper commitments. He used to live with a dude who screwed him out of money who he later found screwing his best friend. After that, we never heard of him in another relationship, not even a casual fuck. He likes hanging out with friends, drinking good wine, beer and telling stories. He had to leave his apartment in Caballito and move in with his mother in Lanús. It took his father many years to come to grips with his sexuality. Nowadays he's proud of him and happy to see him working on plays or playing with us. A couple of months ago, "15" took him to a gay bar. His dad was surprised that he didn't find the stereotypes that he'd imagined. Since then, they're fixtures almost every Friday at Club Glorias Argentinas where they drink beers, share tapas and talk. They're making up for all the lost years in which they didn't even talk on the phone. Coming out to him lifted a considerable weight off of his shoulders and it's been good since.

A while back, while drinking wine, his dad told him:

—Did you see my buddy José María? Well, you won't believe what he confessed to me the other night at the *milonga*. He's gonna leave Carmen because he can't live a double life anymore... he's been hanging out with a little 20-year-old snot... one of his students. I think he thought I was gonna get mad, that I was gonna rough him up and forget him. But no; I hugged him for the first time in our 25 years of friendship! He's been like a brother to me and you have no idea how good it felt for him to tell me. I wanted to bawl but I kept it together.

—It's the tango in you pops...

—After some drinks later, he told me that it had hurt him over the years to keep that from me but I reassured him that I had known all along. I mean, if the guy's happy... who am I to rain on that? It's his loss at the *milonga*, with all those fine bitches begging to be grabbed!

—Maybe he got tired of girls dad... wasn't he always fucking around with them? Wasn't he quite the ladies man? –His cellphone rang. Looking at the caller ID:

—It's mom.

—Answer it.

—Hey. No. I can't now—after a moment of silence—No. Not now. Look, I'll call you later, like in an hour. Ok?

—You know that better than me. You don't go "changing" like that, like you do a shirt. He hid it like you all do at first; and the son of a bitch hid it well, no one saw it coming. But that's between you and me, got it? You can't let something like this out.

—No dad, don't worry about it, I won't tell anyone.

—Though nowadays? Who's gonna bat an eye at that? With what you see... –"15's" cellphone rang again and he answered without looking; it was his mom again and it was the same transaction as before, almost word for word.

They finished their wines and stood up. His dad made a beeline for the *milonga* and "15" went home to sleep. The next day we had a match in Huracán's practice field and they both knew they'd be getting together the following week at the same place.

"15" went to bed and fingered, without much interest, through a Rolling Stone. He stopped when he noticed that he had a hard-on. He spat into his hand and rubbed the thick saliva unto his dick's head. The thought of his old man dancing tangos with other dudes got him hot. He pulled harder on his dick, jerking it off until he passed out. At midnight he told me, he got up to take a piss. When he came back, he found the mattress wet and sticky; his cum humid on the sheets. He remembered when he was a young boy and after waking from horrible nightmares, his old man helping him pee. He laughed to himself, happy, like a five-year-old boy.

## <<16>>
## BROTHER

**1**

He left the pitch bitching at us; kicked off his cleats, grabbed his bag, and crossed the avenue barefoot—he looked like the Incredible Hulk. He came back a few months later and repeated the same scene. Later, he showed up for a training session—he looked like a good boy; quiet, observant—then he vanished. During the following week we noticed he had blocked us on the chat and put our e-mail addresses in the spam folder. He didn't answer his cellphone either. He didn't play with us again.

"16" didn't keep anything to himself; he always said the first thing that came to his mind. He wasn't rational, he was emotional. He was sensitive to any little thing we told him. He was convinced that we didn't take him into consideration and purposefully left him out. He would go around saying that we didn't recognize his efforts within the team but if we praised him, he'd bitch that we were bullshitting him. Beyond his disagreements with Coach, it never came down to fists—his worst offence was throwing his jersey at the face of his sub during a game. That was "16," he was a lot like Grouchy Smurf but from day one we nicknamed him "The Fury."

On a train ride from Washington to Pennsylvania, I told him he was too emotional; that he needed to take pause and think before he acted instead of getting enraged and vomiting his anger at us. When he got up to use the restroom, he told me:

—I'll be back, bro. —I liked that, being called "bro," made me feel like a friendship was taking hold. As time went by though, I began to notice that the sobriquet had a different meaning.

"The Fury" never met his pops, didn't even know who it was. Didn't have any brothers. He was 32 and into 20-year-olds. He liked hoods and gangbangers; the way they dressed in baggy sweats, ball caps, thick sneakers and who listened to cumbia and reggaeton. If they were poor and and at odds with the law, even better. He found them jobs, lent them cash, bought them hamburgers and beers when he brought them around.

## 2

One Sunday, he went with me to buy some weed in Ciudad Oculta, where his boy's rival gang lived. I heard him say as he pulled a blade: –If they mess with him, I'm gonna fuck them up, you hear?

The dark-eyed hood who had beat the living shit out of "The Fury's" boyfriend was indifferent to him. "These shits have nothing to lose. The cops are into them, they don't have a fly's dick to suck," said "The Fury" as we walked through the villa. To get into the gang, his boyfriend had gone through the initiation rite which involved getting fucked by the three leaders. His boyfriend, Patricio, had hooked up with the hood and fucked him secretly at the factory where he worked. After they stopped and it turned into hurling insults, he took an air of indifference towards him. Patricio started insinuating that the dark-eyed hood liked his big ole dick. The fight started with a flurry of spitting and ended with Patricio tied to a tree, with the dark-eyed hood pissing on him in front of everyone. He bumped into him after that, on the Chicago stands. Patricio was alone but he wasn't afraid of him. He said hi like he had done before and they sat together throughout the game. Afterwards, he motioned him to one of the bathrooms. Later that afternoon, as they exited through Cárdenas Avenue, the hood got shot on the shoulder. He found out later that he had an enemy and a protector. The guy who shot the hood had been one of the three who fucked him during the initiation. His name was "Merengue" and he was fair skinned, like an egg's white. He was handsome, tall and clear-eyed. He was shacked with an 18-year-old Paraguayan chick who had a great ass and swung it around when she walked making all the boys go crazy. They had three kids together, with a fourth on the way—but he still had a hard-on for the hood and was crazier now for him more than ever since they stopped fucking.

"The Fury" had helped Patricio leave the villa and open up a kiosk near his home. In the mornings, he supplied him with boxes of merch he'd bought in bulk from a distro in Once. My friend liked looking at his boy naked, his white ball cap on backwards, the blue sweats that framed his bulge and the faded Argentine national team jersey that he never took off. He liked the smell of his armpits, his balls. Patricio had gotten a green and black shield, Chicago's logo, tattooed on his chest; and another one with "The Fury's" initials on his ring finger so as to fudge "Merengue's" "M." But he was still messing with that hood who could care less about him.


3


When I bumped into "The Fury" at the Gay Pride Parade, he invited me to drink a beer and he told me about his new trophy: "Correntino." I knew "The Fury" well enough to know this story would play out over two or three months and it would end in rage and anger, like they all did before. When he left, he hugged me and said:
—Brother –but this time he added –My man, have you figured out this "brother" thing yet or what? –That left me wondering. I ran through different scenarios; wild and disparate. Were we sons of the same dad? I discarded that immediately due to its absurdity. Was "The Fury" falling in love with me? I wasn't skinny. I wasn't a fucking hood rat and I hadn't been 20-years-old in a long time. I laughed at that. But then I thought: "Is he my bro because we share things? Is he homeless and wants to move in with me?" But none of those made any real sense to me. I was baffled.

4

He called the new hoods he met "pups" and loved petting them like he was rubbing his dick. Some of those boys didn't talk—they were either too timid or drugged out. Others, he put up on an altar, lauding them for their rural beauty. "The Fury" had a natural affinity for these downtrodden kids.

—Facu, the thuggier and more suffered these guys are, the more submissive they're in bed. It's amazing!

—Where do you find them? I asked. It had been something that I had wondered for a while; the other thing that intrigued me, the "brother" thing, would come later.

—On the school's pitch man. I hook up there like crazy. When they chant "take it up the ass" and shit like that, it's real Facu. It's a different world there... how long has it been since you've gone by? Did you ever go?

I was running late to an exam at school but I knew I'd see "The Fury" in training the next day. He missed Tuesday. Thursday's game was postponed due to rain. I bumped into him on Saturday during a friendly in Ezeiza. He was bitching that Coach had left him out of the Sunday roster. He was saying that no one took his efforts seriously; how he had served "11" some incredible assists. Then he got angry at the food we were given—that the chicken was raw and there was too little of it, that the lettuce tasted like dirt because they didn't wash it right, and that the mashed potatoes were a notable absence on his plate. He launched into a tirade against the "son of a bitch ref" who had yellow carded him at his last game while he ate. While he peeled his apple, he bitched about them buying them green since they were cheaper than the red ones. Then he started on "7."

—He never passes the ball, egotistical bastard. He never includes me in the plays, in anything. Look at the little shit –motioning with his arms –he even eats alone too! When we were done eating, I got up and shook his hand:

—See ya brother.

His eyes got big and shiny.

—Aha! You figured it out? –he asked somewhat taken aback. I winked at him and went to take a nap under the shade of a tree. A few minutes later, he was kneeling beside me, resting his forearm on my leg. He started talking about this kid Braian he had met while riding bike near Diego's place in Fiorito. Braian worked as a stock boy at a supermarket in Lanús. He took care of his mom and brothers. He liked Marley. "The Fury" had a bracelet with Rasta colors with a rainbow flag one below it around his wrist.

—Guess which song the pup likes the best?

—…

—"Iron Lion Zion" and "Africa Unite." He hates "Woman," just like me! The pup's just like me! He only smokes a little weed and doesn't fuck around with the police, this one's for me! You can't even begin to imagine the back on him and how sweet he is. We spend the evenings doing nothing, just holding each other, quiet. His skin is so soft. He holds me tight. He smells delicious Facu, he's so beautiful and he showers me with kisses: on the face, my chest, my legs, my back, on my balls, everywhere… the pup's divine.

—Brother? –I asked. His face lit up. –Why do you call me brother? What are you trying to tell me? –all at once.

—Oh man, you beat me that time on the train, remember? A truth? Really? Bah! Whatever, I'll tell you another one… you sure you didn't figure it out?

—No…

—Well, go and ask "12," he'll tell you. You know what the pup asked me? If I wanted to move in with him. He's got a huge room and he misses me at night. This pup's for me, there's no more thought to it Facu. He's for me!

—How old is he? –I asked as I texted "12."

"12" didn't miss a beat and answered immediately: "He calls you 'brother' because you both sucked on the same cock." Now I've gotta find out whose cock that was.

## <<17>>
## PLASTIC DREAMS

I told "4" to close the window, it was cold. The highway turned into Ricchieri and later, into General Paz. We were on our way to Saturday's training, but it felt like a Sunday. From the stereo blared CumbiaGei's "Piola Petero." The song finished and started again, burning our ears. "9" and "4" traveled in the front seat. "3" was on top of "8." The sub keeper, "7" and "9" were behind; "17" had sat on top of me. When my legs cramped, I opened them and "17" fell in-between. I grabbed onto "17's" waist and he didn't say anything. The guys sang the song and applauded. When it was over I bent, as far as I could, forward, pressed "stop" and then "play." The CD started again. This time it was "I Fit the Guys." I leaned my head on "17" and closed my eyes. I remembered what we told each other over breakfast.

While we waited for the missing guys to arrive, we drank *mates* with scones at "9's" house. "17" told us his dream:

—I was alone with the ball. Later, I realized that I was not alone fter all, you were there and it was raining. It was raining a lot. But it was not cold. We ran through the countryside. We ran like Coach tells us not to run. He was not there. And suddenly we started kicking hard, splashing the water. We splashed everything, without wanting to. The land was transformed into a paddock. Grass flew through the air. It was a nice feeling.

When I heard what "17" had dreamt, I was surprised. I was going to say something but I stopped... I asked myself if they were going to believe; then I thought that they were my friends, that we lived through a lot of things and that there was no reason to think that I could lie to them:

—Fuuuuc... You won't believe me. I swear, on my boyfriend's cock which is nice, that I dreamt the exact same thing.

—Noooooooooooo.

—Yeah fucker. We were in a place, like Cantillo, but it was not Cantillo. We had new shirts, soaked with water, and you started showing off with the ball in the middle of the game. I have that image in my head as if it were a moving photo. They marked you, but they couldn't get it from you. And yes, it's true, there was mud and grass flying in the air... you know what? Let's call J. and he can tell you. When I woke up, I told him the dream. Let's put the phone on hands-free and you'll see I'm not lying.

—Nah, man. No need. We believe you.

—Yeah, we believe you —they told me again and they passed me the *mate*. It didn't have sugar. I drank it anyways. The tea, which he had left on the table, had cooled. At that moment I felt the presence of "17." The boys talked and we looked at each other. There was a complicity that led us to think the same:

—How can it be that two people have the same dream? —I asked myself.

—There are things that are. They are... incredible, —said "17" softly into my ear.

I thought something and he put into words what I had thought. When I changed the song and rested my head on his shoulder, he sighed and began to stroke the back of my neck. Then he told me:

—Connection. We're connected. But, it can not be explained — the keeper interrupted— I can't take it anymore, dude. Last night I had some vodkas, half a bottle of watermelon liquor that was awful; and now, between the *mate* and the sweets and this shitty back and forth... I can't take it anymore.

—But... stop dude... You can't hold it a bit? We're almost there...

—Blaaagh —he echoed dryly. Someone instantly handed him a roll of toilet paper. Another guy had lowered the window and pushed him through it. We stopped on the side of the road, by a drop in the rollercoaster road that took us unto dirt. After five minutes, more or less, we drove off. The keeper had not vomited. Couldn't. They even offered to put fingers and dicks down his throat, but he did not want to.

"3" passed the joint. I grabbed it. Some bitched about the smoke in the car. I kept leaning on "17," thinking, but I do not remember what.

He had not stopped stroking the back of my neck. He had not taken his hat off either. He lifted his shirt. I saw his cut abdomen. I stroked his belly. His skin was soft. How couldn't it be, if he had not yet turned 21? Until a few months ago he had a girlfriend. "Tubérculo" had taken him to play with us. Like he had told us, he was straight but wanted to try. He had told me that he did not want to have sex with some bum, but to be naked in the pastures of the pitch, to hug and nothing else. We stopped for two minutes. While pissing next to the keeper, I saw how "6's" hand grabbed "17's" dick. He helped him draw with his pee. When the joint hit me I thought of J. He had been working for several months. He did not have time for anything and lived in a bad mood. We didn't have a lot of sex. I'd jerk off two or three times a day. We got back in the car. When "17" gave me the joint, we looked at each other again. Our eyes met. We did not say anything, but we knew what we were thinking. We looked through the window. The sky had darkened, it looked bruised. The rain needed to end in order to erase the differences between dreams and what we were living, between gay and straight. I thought we could be two people who became one. "Man stuff. Manly things," said "17," softly again, into my ear, guessing my thoughts. He was breathing on my neck. I felt his breath. Until that moment I did not believe in the mystical, magic, or in destiny. But something was making me think differently. When we got there, we went straight to the dressing room. We changed and left the bags in the lockers. We had a meeting. The team captain coordinated it. He showed us a video with strategic plays. When we left it was noon and there were no clouds. The keeper was doing tricks and the ball bounced on his foot as if it had a magnet. The others ran around the pitch. "17" left the group when his cell phone rang, which he had left next to the goal. I got close, stealthily, and listened to the conversation. It was Mara, his ex. They were going to see each other that night. He told her:

—I love you, baby. I'm gonna suck your pussy like never before.

I dropped the bottle of water I was drinking. I was out of energy. I looked at him and saw him differently. He was ugly, and prettier than ever; but it was not the same as before. I thought about fucking up his face. I held back. My cellphone rang. It was J. He told me he missed me.

He asked me if I wanted him to pick me up with his car and then go to dinner.

The shirts were soaked with perspiration. Some of us ended up playing naked. I remembered my dream and "17's." It had been a long time since I had played under such a strong sun, it looked like a tomato. No signs of any rain either.

*Winning wasn't as good as losing. Losing made us focus on fixing difficulties. Winning fed our egos. After the "pro" matches we all went our own ways, thinking higher of ourselves; like we had contributed immensely to the match.*

## <<18>>
## FAMILY

"18" used to come to scrimmage with his dad who was a blacksmith. They worked together at the same mill until Antonio got laid off during the big labor purge of 2008. Antonio had split from his wife and they lived alone—since she stopped coming around to see "18" after they broke up. His unemployment had them both worried. He wasn't that good at soccer to begin with and the added worry made him worse. Whenever Coach would scold him or tell him what to do, his old man— always within earshot of our bench—would get all worked up over it. You could see it in his eyes; wanting to jump in and stand up for him. He'd whip out a cigarette and smoke it instead.

"18" told me that he'd joined the team because his old man brought him over in order to show him that fags were all the same— effeminate cross-dressers. But from day one they found out we weren't like that and his old man was so impressed and taken aback by it that he was friendly and helpful towards us. It was like he brought "18" to his first day of school and was more interested in the homework load than his own son.

"18" was 20 by the time he joined the team. He was tall, skinny and stringy like a green bean, and baby-faced too. His beard hadn't filled out yet. His ball cap was attached to him, whether he was playing or not; and he always carried around the same kit bag his dad had. He treated his cleats like a cherished girlfriend and kept them polished and shiny. He was thinking about going back to school, take night courses. At the mill, he got into an argument with his supervisor when he wouldn't change his schedule so he could practice with us. "18" didn't take it well and told him to go fuck himself up the ass. That got him pipelined to the top of the list for the next round of layoffs which took place exactly two months later. He never got around to signing up for those night courses.

He wasn't seeing anyone; neither boy or girl and there was a rumor going around that he was a man on the pitch but a little bitch outside of it. He told me about his first time. It had been on a summer night, after drinking a few beers on the balcony of his house. A little before dawn, he went to sleep on his old man's bed. He had closed the windows that faced the street and turned on the ceiling fan. Five minutes later, Lucas was on top of the bed. Lucas lived on the same floor, down the hall from him. At first, he felt the slight brush of their bodies touching; their beer breaths colliding. Their mouths met. For the first time, in the 20 years of knowing each other, they embraced and didn't let go. They fucked. First one, then the other; like some kid's game. They stayed like that, inside each other without moving until the sun began to creep in through the blinds. They fell asleep and without the will to wake, or pull apart; they did so, rather violently, when "18's" dad came into the room. He saw them naked, on top of each other as if they were one body—cock to cock, a phallic helix—their arms and legs entwined also. They didn't want to wake from that.

Lucas' folks sent him away to Entre Ríos, to live with some relatives. The boys, who were also distant cousins, texted each other all day long until they ran out of data. As time went by though, passions cooled considerably but "18" could never forget his cousin and he never sought the company of another person. He remembered Lucas' warm dick, the crack of his armpits and his toes—all which he sucked on until he fell asleep. Before that night, they had sat together on the street corner: their legs up against each other, like a secret code bonding them in front of the other kids.

A couple of days after the incident, "18" was making himself a cup of *mate* while trying to explain to his old man that he wasn't gay; that he and his cousin had just been watching internet porn and had been jacking-off. It was the first time they had talked like this. He told him how it happened: how one had touched the other with the condition that he'd touch back after. He promised his dad that he wouldn't ever do that again with another boy.

He couldn't stop thinking about Lucas, who was his same age, went to the same school as he and lived in the same building. His cousin had gotten off the chat and had stopped responding to his texts. That aside, he continued believing that his cousin would think about him too.

After listening to "18," *mate* after *mate*; he told him the real reason as to why he'd split with his mother. He'd caught her in bed fucking his brother. "18" was surprised, but downplaying it, he confessed to his dad that in the time leading up to their split, he had stopped relating to her—that she'd confuse him with Antonio—and reproached him for it. They laughed earnestly about it, the conversation ending when one of them got up to empty the *mate* leaves from the teapot and said:

—Women… –while moving his head like a bobble-doll. They never talked about it again.

The team had a trip to Entre Ríos pending. "18" got called up to the roster by Coach as a sub. His old man, apologizing for their economic situation and using his pride as an excuse, forbade us from putting up cash for his expenses and told his son, in front of the whole team, that if he was going on the trip, to not bother returning home.

From that day on, we never heard from "18" again. He didn't travel with the team and he never went home either. His old man kept going to see us train and play. One morning, after we asked about "18," he said:

—Watching you kids play, is like watching him. Fuck, he had raw talent, too bad he was so impulsive… the son of a bitch could've gone far. But whatever; you guys won't let me down… –as he threw away a half-smoked cigarette onto the freshly mowed lawn. "7," who works at a temp agency, is very close to getting him a job at a factory.

## <<COACH>>

The day we played nude, it poured. The pitch was a muddy mess. In some parts it was like a well, in others like an Olympic pool. It was terrible but we were enjoying the game. The ball got stuck a lot and booting it around was a challenge. The cleats couldn't grip and we were slipping and sliding the whole time. Instead of kicking the ball, we were splashing water around, blinding the opposing players with a cascade of shit. For a brief second, a rainbow formed behind a booted ball. It was impossible, the sky was black and it was thundering and lightening. It was crazy, our movements framed into slow-motion with the atmospheric strobe lighting. All of our movements were calm, like some movie we were starring in was beginning to catch speed. It was surreal— we felt our bodies hot, expanding, searching each other out like strings falling into place on a fabric matrix, a work of art. This image vanished from my mind into a watershed of colors. In the meantime, we kept playing and taking in, strangely enough, the weird conscience of who we were, where we were, what we were doing, what was the point of being there, the time we had been playing. Every ball exchanged was as if a little bit of ourselves broke off and was shared with others. Every challenge with the opponent a new opportunity to rediscover who was next to us.

The shouting: slow it down, pass it, son of a bitch, over here over here, kick it remained an echo in the first half, right when the first drops began to fall. When someone passed the ball, they'd say:

—Buddy, you owe me... –the debts suddenly unrepayable. "3" said we owed him 58 blowjobs while he himself owed 55 without ever repaying a single one of them.

In the second half, under the effects of the anisette; there were no more screams, no more joking, no more mooning the other team— everything was driven by passion now and a little sense of order. "13" had a sudden impulse. "7" followed him and he in turn was followed by

"4" and "5" — one by one, the whole team was buck naked under a curtain of rain.

The water came with an unstoppable and never-ending fury. It was hot and aside from us, there was no one else at the park. It was at that moment, while we took ourselves in playing on that field, naked and under thick rain clouds that looked like blood sausages, that someone finally said:

—We're doing this 'cause Coach isn't here –and I remembered what my psychologist had told me:

—Don't fire the coach, beyond what little problems you guys might have with him, he's your technical director; he's your law and he sets the boundaries.

At that moment, that question crashed against the heavens, prompting a meteorite rain that pelted us in the form of more questions questioning everything. Coach had been a cop and then a corrections officer at a jail. He put in 20 years on the queer wing of the prison. He never wanted to tell us what he witnessed there beyond:

—There are things that happen, unimaginable things… and there are other things you don't repeat… not everything can be told –he concluded. Those words swirled around in my head. I imagined things.

"9" threw himself atop the clothing mound we had erected next to the goal. He was thinking to himself; his arms and legs spread-eagle. He was looking at the sky, hyper-perceptive as it began to clear. The stars appeared like celestial cream puff bomb flashes.

I lost track of time and a bit of my memory. I can't, for the life of me, remember anything that happened after. I'm missing so many links from that night. All I remember, as I looked at the ceiling, clothed, in my bed before falling asleep is that in the early morning we ran a practice drill version of take-away, "the nut."

It involved us getting even more naked, while the "nut" ran around trying to take the ball away from us (ran around in a sense, everything was still in slow-motion then). Whoever had the ball would say the first thing that came to mind as they dribbled the ball. That's how "5" said:

—I have too much of an ego. I wanna dribble by all of you and have everyone applaud me by taking it from midfield all the way and scoring. Me, me, and me. I have a hard time having to pass the ball. I have a hard time not thinking about myself…

"8" stepped on the ball and fell. He almost fell backwards. "6" saw the ball roll out and made a try for it. He *moved* like he was running, but he hadn't moved an inch. "8" finally got control back, he made a couple of fancy moves and started talking:

—I can't believe how much my life changed after I met this dude… he's a pal –he… he… he… when I'm with him, I don't even think about sex, I only wanna be with him… if I coul… coul… ("8" was talking like he was in a dream) if I could p, p, p –lay… Play. It's like he had just discovered the word "play." Play. And if I, I could concentrate. Concentrate. Concentrate on my game on the pitch, in sync, like when I'm with Jonathan, I think I'd be eight times better than I already am. My problem is sex. Sex. Sex. Sex controls me. I take one look at a rival's bulge and I lose my concentration. I'm thinking about it all the time… – and as he looked at the "nut" making a wild play to get the ball from him, he made a quick flick of it to "3." He rubbed his chest in circular motions. He looked like the dying screen of an old TV as the colors faded to black. In an instance, his hands were crossing through him, side to side, like a giant hole had appeared on his body.

—As "3" brought the pass under control, he said:

—I was born to defend. On the pitch I don't care about a goddamned thing. The ball must not cross my area. That's my job. When I do my job, I feel like He-Man. I'd kill a motherfucker so the ball doesn't net… that's my only goal in life. I was born to defend: even back when my dad used to beat the shit out of my mom; I can't believe I'm saying this. It's amazing what I've learned with you lot… I love you guys! –he no-look passed it to the guy in front of him. "4" got it, he too had a giant hole in him and he shined like a CD.

Everyone kept confessing while the "nut" kept running after the ball; until finally exhausted, he threw himself unto the grass to look at the orange sky which had opened like a giant conch from which we all fell. We jumped and bounced a thousand times. We didn't feel the cold, or the heat, or tired. Everything was in perfect balance. Everything was perfect.

I don't remember anything else. Only that I saw myself like I was something or someone else, drinking at the water fountain in the locker room—drinking and drinking without stopping. I don't know if it was seconds or minutes; it felt like an eternity. I couldn't stop discovering new things, or how awesome the water felt on my skin. I don't even know how I got back home.

The following week, one of us—we never found out who—called Coach asking him to recheck his attitude but to be cool and rejoin the team. The rest of us wondered if we needed him at all.

# THE END

Facundo R. Soto is a narrator, novelist, poet and psychologist as well as an avid football (soccer) fanatic. His poetry collections include *Microondas* and *Olor a pasto recién cortado*. Facundo was born in Buenos Aires, Argentina in 1972.